200 beats per minute

200 Beats per Minute
A Novel by Eddie Beverage
ISBN 0-9664297-0-2
LCCN 98-85763

Sure Shot Publishing
PO Box 622257
Oviedo, FL 32762

Printed in the United States of America

This novel is dedicated to my family
and friends.

For your love and support, I am eternally grateful.

Eddie Beverage

"To be nobody but yourself in a world which is doing its best, night and day, to make you everybody else, means to fight the hardest battle which any human being can fight, and never stop fighting."

ee cummings

"All the world's a schoolyard, all the people merely pushers."

Danny Boyle

Introduction

Hello Friends. Danny Boyle here. I'd like to start out by saying that I love every last one of you. We're going to be spending quite a bit of time together this week, and it's important to me that you know this. For better or worse, I love you, and I understand. I really do.

Times are changing and I know it's not easy. Unfortunately for most of us, as the naiveté of childhood fades, so do our illusions. Gender roles. Religion. Politics. The corporate ladder. I don't know about you, but I'm pissed that I didn't have a say in any of it. The scariest part is that none of these issues even begins to speak to the way we treat each other. Discrimination. Violence. Hate. The human race has made tremendous strides in so many arenas, but when it comes to each other, we just can't seem to get it right.

For a long time I thought I was alone. I considered my dreams of a different way, a better way, to be idealistic fantasies, the silly sentiments of "the kid who could change the world". Then I attended my first rave and realized that I was not alone. It was there that I was introduced to P.L.U.R. — Peace, Love, Unity and Respect.

The ethics of P.L.U.R. are nothing new. Every generation has embraced similar ideas in their own way, but we must not succumb to the demons of those who have gone before us; elitism, in-fighting, drug abuse. I'm afraid to say that when these words reach you, the backlash will have already begun. For too long it has been assumed that the nobleness of the cause *alone* will carry it. The old adage of building castles in the sky comes to mind, and now that it has come time to build a foundation, we have lost sight.

To me, the problem is clear; it's the solution that escapes me. Any ideology with roots in a "scene" decays over time, especially if those roots are not nourished. Not only have we failed our roots, they are being hacked away, bringing that ideology down on our heads.

Raves have become fashion shows. Drugstores. Too many kids with blinders on. Too much to prove. Phat sneakers take precedence over phat vibes. House rules over house music. Drugs over love. And all of this, while the true enemy, the media, stands in the wings, a bag of salt thrown over its shoulder, patiently eyeing our wounds.

Though they are intent on attacking us for it, what the media and other groups have failed to realize, is that drugs are everywhere, a symptom of a much larger problem. In a sense, they're are a symptom and the cure. Kids want relief. A way to ease the pain. A back door to a world that shuts them out even as it closes them in.

We live in an addictive culture. Unfortunately, there is a lot of money at stake and in the best interest of corporate America to keep it that way. Kids and people in general too often turn towards their vices rather than acquire coping skills. Vices are more easily fed by the capitalist machine. It's a marketer's dream. A drug dealer's paradise. A niche that spans all age groups, both sexes and all walks of life. This happens *everywhere*. It's not a rave thing. It's a human thing. It's also a shame, because drugs aren't the answer.

Please do not misunderstand me. My story is not intended to be some sort of straight edge manifesto. I feel that drugs, and the extent to which someone uses them, is a personal choice. The last thing I want is to be remembered as being on some moralistic high horse.

My story is about the head games we play with ourselves. About breaking down the walls. About listening to our hearts and being true to what we believe in. About global healing through *self* healing. I really believe that all the insight that one ever seeks is all right there, in the ebb and *flow* of the subconscious.

There's currently a war being waged within my own subconscious. Good and evil are vying for my very soul as we speak. Besieged on both fronts, I've assumed the role of historian to the bloody battles of my rational mind. It's all documented in my journal, which I'll be sharing with you along the way. I like to think of it as my contribution to the archives of the one great mind, the universal mind; a home for my poetry, soapbox ramblings, chemical musings and assorted other mind candy.

Many of you out there are battling addiction yourselves, struggling with your own identities, sexual and otherwise, and some, simply trying to find their place in this cold, impersonal world. Please know one thing - *you are not alone*. It is my sincere intention that my words will in some way facilitate your own quest for self discovery and awareness. You may identify with my unquenchable curiosity for the world in which we live. With my fascination of the human condition. With my pain and with my joys. On another level, you may relate to my passion for music and dance. To the love that I have for the culture that has embraced me, and I, it. Even to my humorous reflections on the tragic comedy called *Life* playing out all around us.

I believe that at the heart of human understanding is the communication of shared experiences. I suppose if my story says anything about where we've been and where we're headed, it's that it's all right to be confused. It's all right to *not know*. Now that the Information Age is upon us, there seems to be pressure, more than ever, to be "in the know." I say fuck that. I say scream *I don't know* from the highest building you can find.

Anyone who isn't confused and absolutely bewildered by the world in which we live is either, one, lying to you, or two, simply not trying hard enough. So make them work. Force them to own up to humanity; to their fellow mortals. Make them believers. If not you, then who?

All I ask in return for the story that I am about to share is one small favor. As to the bigger picture, I believe it's a puzzle, and each of us holds a piece. When you're done reading, please share your piece with the world.

My piece? You're holding it.

1
5:30 am, Sunday morning

The dance floor is abuzz with the pre-dawn euphoria that every club kid lives for, the crowd an eclectic mix of neo-punks, skaters, ravers and misfits. All walks of life are represented. Represent poor. Represent wealthy. Represent urban. Represent rural. Represent black. Represent white.

Me? I'm not representing too righteously right now. I lost the rest of the guys about two hours ago, right around the time I lost my mind...out of my head on acid.

Ecstasy would have been nice, but I didn't have the cash for a pill. I could've borrowed money from Chad, or Jason...such thoughts have been drag racing through my mind like two maxed-out Chevy Novas charging and passing on a dark, deserted road...*yo Danny how's it hangin?, chill, you?, fucked up?, who, me?, yeah you, a pill, no acid's cool, no way, fucked up, no shit*...been so speeded out I can't think straight.

Sweaty palms. Dizzy. Nauseous.

I shouldn't feel this way, but panic is your worst enemy. Just chill and ride it out I tell myself.

I picture a sunset in my head. The waves rolling into a beach on a secluded island. The sand between my toes. Fresh air. Then the sun melts into the sea turning the water blood red, crabs in the sand, the air gets thin.

I shake my head, erasing the image, like from an Etch-a-Sketch. I can hear my brain rattling around inside, like it's become detached from my spine, toppling end over end; a tiny washing machine in a terminal spin cycle. It's deafening. Cut to the DJ.....

..he's about ten feet above the dance floor, the lights outlining him prophetically in his booth...my mind plays cut and paste like so, one moment in turmoil, captivated in the next.

Conjuring images of a demonic puppeteer manipulating a marionette, skillfully pulling the strings of the crowd, my admiration quickly turns to envy — I long for such control. My life has been slipping away from me ever since my dad passed on....

...and my head is going to go there, no matter how hard I fight it.

I distinctly remember the smell of crap alongside bed-pan antiseptics and the way the nurse spoke to my mother in hushed tones.

I remember sitting in an uncomfortable chair in a dark corner, legs pulled close to my chest, listening to the heart monitor for hours at a time.

I would try to think of things to say to him, to make it all better, but even as the words came, I somehow knew I would never have the chance to say them.

There's a certain horror, a dread, to losing someone that close to you that must be experienced to be understood. Especially at such a young age, there's only so much support and empathy my peer group could provide. Many had never been in the same position themselves. They would watch people die every night on TV, but then they would drink their Ovaltine and go to bed.

I don't say that in a bitter way. You can't really expect people to understand, but that doesn't bring any comfort. There is no comfort in death. Only pain. And loss.

His liver finally failed him at the young age of 55, a good man and admittedly a heavy drinker, eaten alive by cancer, not just of the liver, but of the soul.

He was never able to express his need to make it all go away, but I suppose whatever it was, the bottle eased his pain, as drugs do for me.

I walk the finest of all lines, that between use and abuse. The ominous chasm of self sprawls out beneath me on both sides, one beset by light, the other by dark. I struggle to comprehend the paradoxical nature of the dark, so warm and inviting.

Somehow I am always able to rationalize it all away, like there's some grand, noble reason for it all.

Metaphorically, drugs are a system of checks and balances to the reality that was fed to me from the day I was born; a reality that has served only as rhetoric for my conscience. After all, what does one who's never been in altered state have to offer as comparison to their so-called reality? The scientific method requires the use of a control group - in a sense, drugs serve as a control group to the great, big experiment called "life", going on around me. A comrade in my ongoing quest for objectivity.

"You all right?," a concerned kid asks me, his eyes rolling back into his head like cherries in a slot machine.

11

"Yeah, fine..," I insist. "You? Blowin' up?," I ask as if there was any doubt.

"The pills goin' around tonight are money, bro."

"That's what I hear," I say, mentally kicking myself again.

"What are you on?," comes the million dollar question.

"Shit-ass blotter," I confess.

"Bad news, bro, those egg shell blotters. Ultra-sketchy right?"

"Yeah."

"That's hated." Thanks for the encouragement I think to myself. As he starts to walk away he thrusts a hand bill at me for a party next week in Tampa called TranceSend.

"I'll be out of town but..thanks," I say, but he doesn't hear me. He's talking to an Asian girl in the corner now. Her shirt says 'Pro Choice.' She's holding a wire hanger in her hand. There's a boy dancing next to her, waving glow sticks wildly. His shirt says 'Jesus Saves.'

For the next half hour or so, I watch my brothers and sisters come and go in front of me, my extended family clothed in a dizzying array of counter culture wares, wallet chains dangling from oversized Fresh Jive jeans, Adidas visors topping off sweaty buzzcuts and dark sunglasses hiding synthetic stares.

Many have been standing around nervously for the past several hours waiting for the right time to eat that first pill, now waiting anxiously for the initial rush, that tingle that whispers quietly unto their soul, *oh yeah*. Artificially induced bliss. Love doves. Tic- tacs. Wafers. Smurfs. Moons. Shamrocks. Floaters. It's all the same to this crew. Ecstasy. And it's all good.

There's a circus theme tonight. I think they're calling it "Big Top." Each room of the club is supposed to represent a different ring of a three ring circus, each ring a different DJ and vibe; all acid jazz in the chill out room, all jungle upstairs, and the mega-mix here in the main room showcasing a variety of styles..hardcore, deep house, acid, tribal, trance.

Even in the midst of the melee occurring in my brain, I can't help but grin subversively at the schizophrenic beats. Somehow the music is always there to bail me out; to get me by. I don't know what I'd do without it.

It seems that there's common core to all music - angst; underneath the words, the genres and the personalities, is angst.

I pity anyone that remains untouched by the emotions behind the sound, unable to hear through the music and visit the mental space occupied by the artists, indifferent to such a heart felt expression of the culture in which we live.

Music builds bridges. It unites. Communicates. Pacifies. Motivates. It changes the way we dress, think, feel and live our lives.

It also turns some of us into fiends who can't get enough and so we dance.

All night.

Welcome to the world of the breakbeat generation.

2

I ate my first hit of acid two years ago. That's when it all started. At first, I didn't know what to think. How is one supposed to react when everything they've ever known is suddenly turned inside out? Then I hit the groove. That one moment during a trip when you feel omnipotent. That moment when everything all of the sudden makes perfect sense. That moment when you can't wipe the smile off your face no matter how hard you might try. Chemical awareness. Flashpoint. Ground zero. I never looked back.

To trip is to leap into the cosmic stream, a stream where one finds the intelligentsia of the ages manifested on a higher plain of consciousness. Walking out across this plain, one is bombarded with libraries full of information, centuries worth of wisdom and insight, an existential treasure trove closely guarded by an army of psychedelic travelers. All who walk the plain, leave their mark and contribute in some way to the greater whole. Only those willing to surrender *are pr..y to this knowledge. Ego must be checked at the door.*

Danny Boyle, Rogue Philosopher. I think for a moment about how ironic it is that all this introspection comes from a kid who's been standing around geeking out on the lights all night. Nothing too "cosmic" about that. Then I envision myself sitting contemplatively, with my hand on my chin like the statue of the thinking man, and I laugh. Out loud. At myself. As I often do.

"Ecstasy?" The kid's dressed like a psychotic, raved out clown, complete with makeup, a rainbow colored wig, platform shoes, a frilly tunic and tights, and a small, blinking strobe attached to a red ball on his nose. Ronald McDonald on mescaline. "E's. Twenty a hit. Blow the fuck up," he promises.

"No. Thanks though."

"Well you can't miss me if you decide you do," he reports before disappearing into the shadows - yeah, no shit, I think to myself. I wonder if certain people realize how risky it is to sell drugs to strangers at a club; stupid even. And why me? I always feel self-conscious after a stranger offers me drugs, like I look like a druggie or something.

I find myself lifting my Oakleys from my eyes and resting them on my head, hands in my pockets now, nodding my head, but who am I fooling? - I'm probably the biggest druggie in this joint.

Maybe I'm being too hard on myself, but lately, it's like I can't get high enough, like watching the same movie or reading the same book again and again and the ending is so anti-climatic you want your money back...*wow, I'm pretty fucked up...*

It's almost laughable, except that cartoons are supposed to be laughable, not life...but that's exactly the way I feel. A cartoon; yet I was created and penned by a different artist than the rest of the cast, like I'm not really a freak, just drawn that way, on a transparent cell over a painted setting colored with drug dealers, and lights, and beats, and other freaks. They come and go, yet they're part of the fabric and I'm not. It's unbearably frustrating.

But then again, identity is not a good topic of conversation especially since I hardly have an objective person in myself to converse with and so I sing..*I'm alive, I'm alive, alive, baby I'm alive*..that really faggy house track that I can't seem to get out of my head, and it takes my mind off the game of mental solitaire I've been playing all night.

The DJ's poised to strike. If he plays his cards right, he could turn this place upside down easily.

I've developed a pretty good eye for when a DJ's about to make his move and this kid's definitely about to play his ace; head cocked, one ear to the next track pumping through his headphones, an anticipatory glow on his face, his body language says it all...going to hold out for as long as he can, and then come correct without any warning.

His fingers glide across the record on the platter as he previews his beat mixing one last time through his Sonys, and then he drops it - a white label, magna-funk track from hell, vectors of a breakbeat tearing through the crowd like groove-injected shrapnel from a sonic frag grenade, infecting the flesh of all in its path.

Dance circles break out all about the dance floor, kids in the corner coming to life as he grins with satisfaction and body rocks behind the tables, saluting the crowd for their good taste. I smile knowingly as the throaty song of several whistles pierce the air, the crowd calling back in appreciation.

Moments later, Travis walks up behind me and starts rubbing my shoulders, digging his fingertips into the back of my neck, massaging my muscles deeply, squashing out the tiny pockets of strychnine just under the surface of my skin.

Travis has always been there like that. He has this

knack for knowing exactly what I need when I'm fucked up..almost like he can read my mind. It's the same kind of sixth sense that lovers have...again, I find it easy to rationalize it all away; I tell myself we're friends, and that all friends feel this way, that it's just the drugs talking. But the truth of the matter is, I have a major crush on Travis, and the lines between friendship, love and lust have become increasingly blurred in the last several months.

We've been in this crazy game together from the very beginning, and our friendship has always meant the world to me. I would never dare risk that and say anything, but at times, I feel like I'm coming out of my skin, overcome by an urgent need to be close to him; very close.

At 160 pounds, Travis is slightly stockier than me, but about the same height. I let him borrow my white and blue Adidas jersey tonight. His light brown hair, cut short and close, brings out boyish, yet chiseled features, thick gold hoops dangling from both ears.

He has an adorable little mole on his cheek, and sometimes I joke around with him and call him Cindy, accusing of him having it faked so he can pursue his dreams of becoming a leggy super model. I'm only half kidding when I say that. He really ought to be in pictures.

I've always believed that one's smile is the gateway to their soul. When Travis smiles, he conveys much more than the emotion of happiness..it's like a shower of acceptance, warmth and understanding, the foundation of that profound connection that we share.

Thoughts of getting in Trav's pants send shivers down my spine..what's left of it anyway; my backbone feels like it has melted away under his fingertips. If only my inhibitions would make the same exit.

"Thanks bro," I say, turning to him. No response, just one of those smiles worth a thousand words. "Where's everybody at?," I ask.

17

"AWOL dude..I can't find anyone. I saw Chad about an hour ago...doing Chad stuff."

Chad Givens, salesman extraordinaire. In order to deal acid, his staple product, Chad will buy a pack of gum, unwrap every piece, place a dose on each and then rewrap them, allowing him to make transactions out in the open. He only deals ecstasy in tablet form, out of an aspirin bottle to avoid too much suspicion, and he's always good for downers too. To many, he's affectionately known as the "ice cream man," scooping ice cream part-time just so he can pilfer the nitrous they use to make whipped cream. From what I understand, he makes a killing on the stuff.

I hop up on a cabinet and pull Travis between my legs, rubbing his neck and scalp as blinding trance bombs rain down around us.

Trav grips my ankles as I rub his shoulders, his arms, his back, then hug him tightly and kiss him on the top of the head. He steps away and turns around flashing that I-know-what-you're-up-to-and-it's-all good smile again.

I jump down from the cabinet and we dance. Before long, I'm exhausted.

"You wanna go round up the crew?," panting, cotton mouth creeping.

"I think we should stay put," he suggests.

"You know Jason, bro. Once he gets his groove on, he'll dance all night. We'll never get out of here."

Dawn is like a promise from an unreliable friend.

Unable to find the space on my mental blackboard to weigh the two alternatives, I concede, leaving Trav to scan the congested dance floor. My throat is beyond dry, it's throbbing, aching, a panicky ache like my windpipe is about to snap.

I project those thoughts at the floor and squash them vindictively with my Pumas as I approach the bar. There's all ready several cups of stale water sitting out for thirsty revelers to snatch up. I grab one, and it tastes like ass, but I can almost hear every cell in my body whisper a collective "thank you". I grab another for myself, one for Trav and begin to work my way back through the crowd.

Somewhere

If sexuality be expressed through longings of the
heart
I am gay
If through the loins
bi
If through my facade
then straight
And if through the truth
Somewhere on the long road in between

3

I make it back just in time to see Chad emerge from the dance floor and embrace Travis. I've been meaning to ask him if he dressed in front of a mirror tonight. He's wearing black Doc Martin shit kickers, camouflage baggies and a wrinkled puke green t-shirt that says 'I'd rather be stoned'. A set of dog tags, *real* dog tags, that his father gave him, hang from his neck. The shirt I can handle, but the rest has to go. It's too militant for my blood. We weren't at war the last I checked.

I shouldn't complain though, war or no war, I'm glad Chad's on my side. He's not the kind of guy I'd want to tangle with in the bush. He just got his head shaved, not slap bald, but close. It tops off 6 feet of lean, mean GI muscle; quite an intimidating look I must say.

As a vet of the scene, Chad usually maintains a poker face throughout the night, calm on the outside, blowing up on the inside. Sometimes its hard to call his poison. Not tonight. Apparently he made enough money on downers in the last hour to treat himself to some coke. He's got that far-off para-

21

noid look. Amphetamine eyes to say the least.

"Yo Dan, can you get my back for a couple minutes?," he asks, rubbing his runny nose with his finger.

"Yeah. What's up?"

"I have to meet somebody in the bathroom upstairs. I'm trying to score some coke for Herbie. I don't know this guy though, just know he has some," he says, lighting a cigarette nervously.

"What'd ya need me for?"

"I don't know the guy Dan. Anything could happen. I just want you to come with me, cool?"

"Think you're being a bit paranoid?"

"Fuck you Danny."

With Chad, coke equals instant attitude problem. He's got a really hot temper when he's flying too. And smokes like a chimney.

He's staring at me wild-eyed now, vigorously trying to massage the coke drip out of his throat. I hand him my water and he swallows it down. "Come on, let's go up top," he says impatiently.

AK1200 is on the decks upstairs representing Florida with some of the fiercest jungle I've ever heard. The rhythm is maddening.

"Keep your eyes open for a punky lookin' blond boy with a Fuct shirt on, O.K.," he screams over the music.

"Yeah," I say nodding.

The bass and the acid double team me, assaulting my senses like a pack of ravenous wolves. The vision in my right eye blurs with every hit of the snare, my left eye on every bass note. "Yeah"...

"Huh?," says Chad leaning towards me.

Jungle music is like a roller coaster ride. Lots of peaks and troughs. Speedy snare drum hits taper off drawing your attention to the bass line, then just when you least expect it, the snares return and the bass line recedes; along comes a lull, no snares or bass, guess again, the bass returns upside your head like a wrecking ball.

"You all right?," Chad asks.

This is your brain.

This is your brain on jungle.

Imagine staring down the ranks of one thousand rabid gibbons charging down a mountainside slinging breakbeats and you're halfway there.

"Danny," he says shaking me...definitely having an episode. The snare track is drilling a hole straight through the center of my brain, coming out at the back of my neck and taking all my sanity with it...no, it stopped...and it's shooting down my spine, raising goose bumps as it races toward my legs, going to come out my feet and track across the floor like a bolt of lightning dragging me with it out over the top of the crowd. I shudder.

"Yeah, fine," I manage.

"Do you see him?"

Visuals abound. Catching trails off the lights up here. They dip, swirl, and rotate, creating phantom like entities to prance merrily before me; a paranormal break dancing frenzy on the floor. I'd close my eyes, but rather than invite them into my head, I pull my shades back down over my eyes.

"There he is," says Chad anxiously, flicking his cigarette to the floor and heading towards the bathroom.

A young, bleach blond boy opens the door ahead of us and we follow him inside. Treble sticks to me like fly paper, then the door slams shut and my ears ring in the silence.

The bathroom is much smaller than the one downstairs. There's one stall, a urinal, a sink and a lock - perfect for all your drug dealing needs.

Chad locks the door behind us and money and drugs change hands quickly. The kid anxiously moves in between us to leave.

"Hold up bro," insists Chad, grabbing the kid by his T-shirt.

"It's good dude."

"I didn't say it wasn't. Just hang out for a second."

Chad methodically sticks a key into the vial and lifts a bump of the white powder to his nose, sniffing it up without hesitation and licking off the residue.

"I told your boy I wanted the same stuff that he got for me. This is crap."

"That is the same shit dude."

"Shit, yes. Same, no."

"Why you sweatin' me?"

"I don't do a lot of coke asshole, but I know what's good. This is garbage."

As the tension mounts, Chad slides his hand into his left front pocket. He's not stupid enough to carry a gun but he carries a tazer with him everywhere he goes. I've never seen him use it on anybody but I know he always keeps it in his left front pocket... "I don't know what to tell you," says the kid reaching for the lock on the door.

"Maybe you didn't understand me. I don't want this," says Chad, leaning on the door.

The tone of his voice puts me on edge..

"Well cut it again and sell it to some other jerk-off."

Chad pounds the kid on the bridge of his nose with the end of the tazer. Twice. His nose opens up on the floor, blood everywhere. Chad lights him up, putting a current to his eyes, his neck, his ears.

Flailing wildly, the kid crashes backwards through the door of the stall and hits his head on the toilet, sprawling out on the tile and flopping around like a fish out of water. Chad kicks him once in the stomach, then grabs the money and a crushed pack of Newports out of his pocket. "Fuck," tossing the damaged smokes to the ground and kicking the kid again.

"Are you out of your mind?," I shout over the music as we walk quickly from the bathroom.

"Guy tried to sell me whack coke Dan, what'd ya want me to do?"

"Well I don't know John fuckin' Gotti."

    My first tazer whipping. A Chad original. Chad lives by the P.L.U.R.F. ethic. Peace, love, unity, respect, now fuck off. It's love thy neighbor, until he fucks thee over. Typical new school mentality.

"Do you have any idea what they cut that shit with?...baby laxative, Dan--I'da been on the shitter all fuckin' night."

"So you break the guy's nose?"

"Who are you, my fucking father?," he sprays angrily.

"What the hell's goin' through your head when you do shit like that?"

"An eight ball, that's what goin' through my head."

"And that's supposed to-"

"And what the hell's that 'sposed to mean..shit like that? Like I'm always doin' shit like that."

"You are. You get a wild hair up your ass and next thing I know, somebody's on the floor. It happens all the time," I say angrily.

    Travis is still standing where we left him, head tilted back, eyes closed, soaking up a new Digweed remix.

"We really need to find Poo and Jason *now*, bro."

"What's up?"

"Dan, would you chill the fuck out. That kid's got like 3 grams of coke on him. They'll haul his ass outta here when they find him," blares Chad.

"Whatever bro."

"He's a dealer. They ain't hearin' his sob story."

"I still haven't seen either of them," responds Travis.

"Man, this acid is fucked up," I say, pacing in front of him.

"Is that good or bad?"

"Right now, that's *bad*."

    Leaving Travis to deal with Chad, I make way down to the edge of the dance floor. Slowly, the music begins to even me out, soothing, trancey fingers caressing my jangled nerves.

If jungle is a roller coaster, trance could be considered a merry-go-round..like the horses on a carousel, trance has peaks and troughs of it's own, but it's much more predictable. As the foundation spins, things remain relatively even up top, repetitive to a point...spinning, the undertow drags me in.

Moments later, though it could have been an hour, my eyes blink open at my name being called from the dance floor. It's Poo. He's swaying back and forth, hands in the air, eyes closed behind large orange goggles, grinning like a dog.

He brought his friend with him tonight, a Grover puppet that his Dad gave him when he was a kid. He pulled the cloth eyes off and re-glued them all crossed up so it looks like Grover is whacked out on some really good E, holding on to him for dear life. It's hysterical.

Poo's real name is Greg. I'll never forget how he earned his nickname. He got loaded on muscle relaxers and Mad Dog 20/20 one night, right before a late showing of *The Wall* downtown, and we had to drag him to his seat.

He slept through most of the movie, then woke suddenly at the end, jumping out of his seat and sitting back down quickly, his face flushed. Greg had shit himself. I never laughed so hard in my life. I saw visions of a tagline in the movie section of the newspaper - "I laughed, I cried, I crapped in my drawers."

Greg's the youngest, a mixed blessing as he sees it. As the baby brother, we're very protective of him, but he also gets picked on a lot. Even if he wasn't the youngest, he'd still be the smallest, an easy target either way. He's only about 5'4" and he can't weigh more than 125, if that.

When he first got his driver's license, he could barely reach the pedals, always on the edge of his seat, clinging to the steering wheel. We would tease him mercilessly. Then he would try to stick up for himself in his thick, Long Island toughguy accent that, considering his size, always made things that much more comical.

"Does one of you pricks wanna drive?"

Laughter.

"What's so fuckin' funny?"

Greg knows we love him though. We took him in when he moved here from New York during our sophomore year - got him laid, got him high, saved him a seat at lunch. In high school, what more could a guy want from a group of friends?

He approaches me shaking his head and grinning, as if nonverbally begging the age-old question, "Wow..are you as fucked up as I am?"

I nod my head.

Just then I realize Chad and Travis have disappeared again. I suppose even if I could get everybody in one spot, our collective brain power approaches zero, so it's fairly pointless. Unanimous decisions are like gold on a night like tonight...I sigh, dying to puff some buds and begin the ride down. My buzz got old real quick tonight. Acid can be such a head trip. Case in point, I turn to Poo and his face morphs on me. "Whoa," I mutter under my breath.

"The room gettin' all flim-flammy on ya?," he asks, snickering at my condition.

Poo's face looks contorted all of the sudden. It's stretched..now skewed to the left..now the right.. "Whoa," again.

Poo can't contain himself and he busts out laughing. I shake my head, whipping the rubbery room from side to side like a dog with a rag doll in its teeth. The walls shimmy like Jello, then settle.

"Better?," asks Poo, giggling mischievously.

"Yeah, but I'm over it.....have you seen Jason?"

I imagine Jason's ears must be burning as he calls out from the dance floor. I tap my watch to let him know we're ready to leave. He's all smiles, dancing with a group of girls. One of them looks like she's having a difficult ride.

I've noticed a lot of that tonight; probably some bad X going around. You never really know what you're going to get anymore. It's only been recently that I started doing ecstasy. Jason first turned me on to raving in January of last year. Back then, the parties were underground and the X was pure.

It appears that the DJ is going to top off his mix with some hard-driving house. Chad and Travis wander back and then decide to join Jason, making one last trip to the dance floor. It's almost 6 a.m. and there's still a line at the front door. For many, the party has just begun.

The garagey snares and DIY bass of a hardcore track has tapered off into a steadier dance beat. Everybody claps rhythmically in time to the music. The house has drawn many people back to the dance floor.

At a rave, dance returns to its roots. It's not entertainment. Not the centerpiece of some tired mating ritual. It's a means of letting the world know how the music makes you feel. Pure expressionism. A device to showcase one's individuality. Self performance art, *primal and necessary*.

Three tracks later, the DJ opens it up and a breathtaking barrage of white noise embraces the crowd over screams of delight and release. His constituents are unanimous in their approval and for a moment, time seems to stand still.

Rapture. Absorb it. Cherish it.
Keep it on the top shelf next to a healthy dose of self-control.

4

My dilated pupils contract, light giving chase as I open the back door of the club. I pull my shades down quickly, cursing the sun on the horizon as it ascends into the sky.

"Whoa. Where are we?," asks Poo, reading my mind.

I have no idea where we parked. From the looks on the faces of my boys, they can't remember either. We all stand in silence for what seems like an eternity, hoping that the lot will magically begin to look familiar. Right now, its alien. It could be any parking lot, anywhere in the world, for all I know.

"Uh..," I protest moments too late as the door slams shut behind us.

This is it. We're on the outside now. No turning back. Suddenly the club doesn't seem like such a bad place to be.

"I can't remember where we parked guys," I admit.

Every car in the lot resembles mine in some way. It's an acid thing - all of them, but none of them, always familiar faces in the crowd. My mind's still playing tricks on me.

As pathetic as it sounds, the bunch of ate-up miscreants that we are, we would get lost and two hours from now we'd still be walking the lot wondering what we were doing there..huh? Oh, Danny's car, that's right.

"Anybody up for breakfast?," suggests Chad.

"Are we just giving up on my car all ready?," I ask.

"Whatta ya got in mind?," asks Poo.

Chad reaches into his pocket, pulls out a set of keys and jingles them around in his hand, smiling devilishly. As if involved in some twisted game of Charades, he feigns dropping a cartridge into an imaginary whipped cream canister, cracking the cartridge and sucking down the tasty gas with glee. So much for self-control, nitrous for breakfast it is.

As we walk, a distant car alarm welcomes me once again to the outside world, the cold steel of a parking meter, an anchor. I check to make sure it's not just a prop, maybe, maybe not - reality is slippery; more cartoon imagery, like in Roger Rabbit, the meter talks back to me.."Keep your hands to yourself, bub"..the car next to me comes to life and begins to sputter like Speed Buggy, the traffic light up ahead screams.."Stop", it's face red with frustration.

"Where the hell you'd get those shoes, bro?," asks Jason, taunting Chad.

"What's wrong with 'em?"

"You look like you belong playing basketball for some third world country or somethin'."

"Fuck you, dude..you and your So Def All-Star Loafers.."

"Yo, the ladies love 'em," Jason giggles, eyes roaming for a new target... "Greg, what up with that girl you been seein'? You hittin' it or what?"

Suddenly the guys are all caricatures with over-large heads, their features smooth and inky and paper thin.

"Who? Kim?"

"I don't know what her name is. The bitch with the gap in her two front teeth, drives that red Geo, really busted grill."

Jason's double reminds me of someone, but I can't pin down the fleeting image.

"Hey, she's got a killer body bro," insists Poo.

"Yeah, I guess. Her mug though, you-"

"She's cool and she likes to fuck, what do you want from me?"

"Your little pee-pee get all caught up in that gap when she sucks your dick?"

Rudy, from Fat Albert, the pseudo homeboy, pants saggin', hat to the back, lazy hip hop stride. Jason is Rudy.

"No," answers Poo.

"Oh really. Mine did," cackles Jason as I stare at him oddly.

"What?" he asks me, annoyed.

There's a group of skaters tricking on the steps of a bank across the street, the clatter of their boards echoing across the cement. A rope thrown from reality's hull, it snaps me out of my spell. "Nothing," I say unconvincingly.

Then one of the skaters takes a fall trying to ride a rail. Jason hollers outs to them - "Maybe next time."

We all have our roles in this game. Me, I'm kind of like the father of this dysfunctional family. Travis is the conscience. Poo, the fuck-up. Chad, the brawn. And Jason, the obnoxious.

I recall a day, several months ago, tripping our asses off at K-Mart. I really can't remember what we were there for. Candy I think. No, it was blank tapes. I wanted to dub some mix tapes off of him. Anyway, he mouthed off to the lady at the cash register. She was taking forever to ring us up; a very pleasant lady, just old and slow.

"How are you boys today?," she asked, her arthritic hands running the tapes over the price scanner several times.

"Fine," trying hard not to stare, tripping out on her rotten teeth. At one point, I actually found myself inside her mouth, like a piece of cabbage stuck between her corroding molars.

"She's got Carpal Tunnel Syndrome or something."

31

"Corporal who's tunnel? That some kind of war injury?"

"Carpal Tunne-"

"What's that got to do with the bitch's hands?"

So she starts entering the price on her own, digit by agonizing digit, and then Jason snatches the tapes out of her hands, punching keys on her register..."price check, price check," pulling the microphone to his mouth and beat boxing obnoxiously for the shoppers in the aisles, rolling his tongue and.."stickum, stickum...", then raises his hands and screams, "Satan loves you all," making the sign with his hand and everything. It was a nightmare.

His shit-talking will get him in trouble sooner or later, but not today. One of the skaters gracefully extends his middle finger at us, while the others scowl.

"Yeah, yeah. Fuckin' posers. Long live the McTwist," he shouts.

When we arrive at the ice cream shop, Chad unlocks the front door, allowing all of us to enter before shutting it and locking it from the inside. In the back room, he cranks the radio. Good radio-friendly rock is always such a treat after being bombarded with house music all night.

"Wait, wait, wait. Turn it back bro."

The new Pantera track. Just what metal needed - a monster groove. Besides being one of my favorite bands, they're a perfect example of feeling music. Yeah, they're loud. Yeah, they're angry. People say they can't relate? Never been angry before? Don't listen to music. Feel it, and relate.

I'm very passionate about music if you haven't noticed all ready. I take my Walkman with me almost everywhere I go..it's like the soundtrack to my life is forever playing in the background. I like it that way, and I have fun with it too; nothing like a little James Brown to put a funky tailspin on my ass when I'm picking up some groceries for mom.

There was a time when my mother was still insisting

that I go to church. Lost your religion? Try this. Go to mass next week and sneak in a cassette player and headphones. Listen to Ministry's 'Burning Inside' full blast during the sermon. Your world will never be the same. You'll swear Christ is about to come down off the cross and fight the battle for good and evil right there in front of your eyes.

I used to play the same game in school, burying my Walkman in my backpack and running my headphones up through my shirt. It's an unbelievably uplifting experience, a rush and a half; something about the juxtaposition of the music to the environment, chaos thriving amidst form, kicking form's ass all over the place, the stillness and order of the classroom versus the unpredictable tyranny of a hardcore track. Me and the guys have dubbed this phenomenon, Schoolhouse Rave..*Sally, Sally, Sally gets her breakbeats here..I'm just a pill, a lonely old pill...*

"Danny, you want anything?," asks Poo from behind the counter.

Cookies 'n' Cream, Swiss Almond Chocolate, Heavenly Hash...everything looks so good, but I don't know if I should eat. My stomach is a little queasy from the acid. I think I'm still tripping too; just caught a nut in the Butter Pecan start hauling ass around the tub out of the corner of my eye, and the Strawberry Cheesecake looks awfully wavy.

Before long, Chad emerges from the back office with a canister, a box full of cartridges and several balloons with the ice cream store's logo imprinted on them. "Breakfast is served boys," he says, cracking the first of the cartridges, unloading it into a balloon and handing it to me.

He does the same for the rest of the guys and then fills one for himself. In silence, we all stand precariously on the brink of the chasm, ready to leap. As a disclaimer, I remind myself that whip-its on acid can be pretty intense.

"Male bonding at its finest," chirps Poo.

Yeah right. I think we all just dig the buzz.

In ritualistic fashion, we exhale until our lungs are empty, raise the balloons to our lips and then inhale and exhale deeply, several times.

The world falls out from underneath me. I drop to my knees and then onto my chest, closing my eyes as colors bombard the canvas on the back of my lids, mostly the brighter ones..red, orange, yellow..purple is oddly present.

I can hear the crew crumbling to the floor around me, and then it *really* hits me. I reach out in an attempt to grab onto something as I feel my body start to spin and levitate up towards the ceiling. The rest of the guys are laughing hysterically, their laughter muffled. Everything's in slow motion except for sound which is accelerated, like an LP playing at the wrong speed. I can't help but cry out, the pitch of my scream wavering like a record that's been in the sun.

All five of us lay, giggling and moaning, our bodies limp with gas on the floor of the ice cream shop. We writhe about for several minutes trying to regain our composure. It takes me a little while longer to get it together.

"You all right Dan?"

"Yeah, fine. Couldn't be better," I reply half-heartedly.

"Oxygen. Oxygen," chortles Poo, feigning a seizure.

"Man, I think I had an out-of-body. My legs were makin' moves for the roof."

"Oh yeah? Your ass put out a contract on 'em?," cackling uncontrollably.

"Yeah, something like that."

Trav's look of concern gives way to an impish smile and he helps me to my feet. I take a seat in the corner next to Poo and Chad. Jason is nowhere in sight. "Where'd Jas go?," I mumble. His voice carries from the back office.

Jason writes rhymes in his spare time, lately that's all of his time..*papahs for the vapahs, who got the papahs? It's Batman and Robin comin' wit' the mad capers..*

I walk to the back as the rest of the guys bring up the

rear. Jason is just about to light the freshly packed bowl of kind bud when Chad grabs his arm.

"In the freezer," he warns, nodding towards the back of the room.

It's the joint, and it should be like that, the splief, and it doobie like that..

"Yeah, well do-be in the freezer bro," says Chad playfully. One by one, we take deep tokes off Jason's pipe. I thank him as I blow a monster hit into the fan.

"It's gonna be a long weekend fellas," I observe on the exhale.

"What's the plan anyway? We gonna kick it at that party tonight or what?," asks Poo, mischievously peeling back the lid on a tub of Chocolate Chip.

"Yo, this ain't the soup kitchen," snaps Chad, smacking Poo's hand as he fingers the ice cream.

Just then, the bells on the front door begin to clatter. Blank faces all the way around, we all look to Chad — "Shit..shit..shit," he exclaims, waving his hands wildly through the smoke.

Stepping out quickly, Chad lets the door close slowly behind him, moving closer to the front of the store to get a better look.

Moments later, the door swings open and he's frantic, waving us out. I feel like Fred Flintstone on the exit. My feet start moving, but my body doesn't seem to respond - Flint"stoned" is more like it. The mental joke makes me giggle and Chad puts his hand over my mouth, scolding me.

We stumble out of the freezer in a THC haze and like cattle, we wait for prodding from Chad who shoves us toward the rear of the shop. Trav opens the back door and we pile into a wide alleyway. "I'll meet you guys down the street," says Chad, hustling back inside.

We run in silence for about a block, then turn a corner, ducking out of sight. Chad arrives moments later.

"I'm fucked dudes," he says between breaths. "That was the owners."

"Why'd you go back in?," I ask.

"To turn off the radio. It's not like it'll make a difference though with the blown whip-its and balloons all over the place."

"Can you say buzzkill? I knew that ya could," pipes Poo jokingly.

"Fuck you Greg. That's my job. I know its frickin' ice cream but shit."

Chad crouches and sinks his head into his hands as I put my hand lightly on his shoulder. "Shake it off, dude. It's all good," says Poo repentingly.

Chad stands up and looks back down the street in a daze. Trav makes a suggestion. "You guys wanna head over to the park and chill for a while?"

I'm starting to come down. My skin is crawling, vibrating; I can hear my pores buzzing, regurgitating the acid. That numb confusion is starting to set in, like my brains have been scrambled, cooked and served up cold to the gods. And I really need to take a shower. Coming down *sucks*. Fuck it. I raise my hand for the park.

5

There's a twisted code of honor that drives the crew. It's as if we show each other how much we care, by the amount of time we spend hanging out and getting fucked up. We will all be going our separate ways at the end of the week, the time we spend together now is valuable and we all know that, but something is wrong. It's never quality time. We never talk about things that really matter-our futures, our families, our friendships.

..as charter members of the "now" generation, our shortened attention spans revel in the urgency of the day. A pension, social security, redemption, eternal happiness..they could all be empty promises as far as we know. My friends are now. The acid in my pocket and the joint in my mouth are now. The music is now.

It's peer pressure I suppose, but it's not like we talk each other into drugs, or give each other a hard time for not doing drugs..well, sometimes..but it's more just like what we know, a commonality, a bond, and nobody seems to want to mess with it. I have faith that there will come a day when drugs will cease to be the center.

The revolution will not be televised..

Trav leads us to the base of a large, secluded oak tree on the outskirts of the park. It's the same spot we've been coming to for years. It brings back memories of a time when skipping school, stealing a case of beer and playing football in the park was living on the edge. We all crash out on the ground under the tree and Jason fires up a fatty. I object.
"Why don't you save that for tonight?"
"Just swing by Deter's place on your way home. We'll get more."
That's one of the problems with drugs. There's *always* more. Somewhere.
"Danny and I are gonna go for a walk. You guys gonna be here?," asks Chad, standing up. The guys nod their heads in unison as I stand to join Chad. "Cool, we'll be right back."
I follow Chad down to the sidewalk that rings the outer edge of the park. We don't speak to each other for several minutes, then he casually breaks the silence.. "I'm sorry if I was being an asshole earlier, bro."
"I'm used to it," I say softly.
"Yeah...I'm sorry for that too."
"Is everything all right? I mean, as stupid as it might sound, I care dude. That's why I get in your face about shit, not cuz I get some kind of satisfaction from it."
"I know."
"So what's up?"
"I talked to Jennifer the other day for the first time since March. She wants me back. Says she misses me. Says she's sorry." I nod to let him know that I am listening.
"Now I can't stop thinking about her again and that can't be.

I have too much else to think about. Shit Dan, I can't believe it's been a year since we graduated. And we've just been jerkin' around ever since. Now I lost my job, my parents have been giving me a hard time, you're going away next week..." His gaze leaves the ground underneath and he looks out across the park.

"I have to get rid of the rest of these doses," sighing heavily.

"I think I can help you with that one," I suggest, winking at him.

We walk in silence again for several minutes. I can't contribute very much support in the relationship arena. I've dated a lot, one girl was semi-serious I suppose, it lasted a pretty intense four months. She stripped me of a sizable chunk of my ego when she left. It hurt pretty bad for a while - I thought, cried, wrote a lot, obsessed a bit, and in the end, I just promised myself never to get so lost in someone else again. That's where the big problems lie, in identity and dependence.

Chad's relationship is co-dependent. His self-esteem has been down since their break-up.

It seems to me that so much needless suffering could be avoided if everyone would take one step back from each other and look inward. Relationships can sometimes become a distraction from dealing with one's self, everyone looking for someone, anyone, but themselves, to blame for their own inadequacies. The question should be, what am I doing here, what is my purpose, who am I? Not, what can he or she do for me, what's their problem, or why won't they accept me? A self-actualized person can then begin to ask, how can I share myself with someone today or how can I contribute to the greater good? It discourages me to see people living through others. So many people attach their own self-worth to their relationships — Chad snaps his fingers in my face and the soapbox in my head explodes. "Am I losing ya kid?," he asks in jest.

"No," I stammer, "no..sorry..just thinkin'."

"And?," he persists.

"You're better off without Jennifer bro."

"It's not that easy though. I love Jennifer, Dan. I never stopped loving her."

Sometimes really cheesy, trite, yet insightful things come to mind and I don't have the courage to say them for fear of sounding stupid. On the verge of suggesting that Chad fall back in love with himself, I digress..

"Well that doesn't justify getting back into the relationship."

"But I need her."

"Can I be completely honest with you for a second? Straight up?"

"Yeah-"

"I don't want you to take this the wrong way, but from where I stand, she fills a hole in your life. You don't need *her*. You need something maybe...but not her."

"Are you telling me to get a life?," he asks defensively.

"I knew you'd take it the wrong way."

"No, that's what you're-"

"Look, I'm not saying I'm Mr. Together...I'm just saying that since Trav and I made plans to go back to school, having a relationship isn't so important to me anymore."

"So, I don't have any goals?," but maybe he's just toying with me. "Is that what you're saying?"

"I didn't say that dude. Don't put words in my mouth." He stops, stares at me for a moment and then goes for my legs. We topple over on the grass and he attempts to pin me. I struggle to roll over on my back.

Before he started using and dealing drugs, Chad was on the high school wrestling team, two-time regional champion even. He's still solid from the days when he would spend hours working out after school and he overpowers me in seconds, kneeling heavily on my outstretched arms and looking me in the eyes until he has my full attention.

"Thanks dude."

"Am I my brother's keeper?," I ask, blood rushing to my head.

"You are your brothers' keeper."

He smiles, grabs me by the hand and yanks me to my feet. I hug him tightly, swatting his ass flirtatiously. We agree that we better head back and round up the fellas. It's late afternoon and none of us has eaten yet, except for the little bit of ice cream at the shop.

I can't help but feel good that I was able to elevate Chad's mood. He's always good about letting me know he appreciates it too. In a way, I think the love that I have for my friends makes up for the absence of a more intimate relationship. It's perfect - they need me and I need them.

On the topic of love, I recall a passage from my journal, written last year. I likened love to a Rubiks Cube. People spend a lot of time trying different combinations, in their search for a solution, or as in the analogy, searching for the perfect relationship.

Individuals approach the cube in a variety of ways. The majority spend hours, days, weeks, even years, tweaking the cube trying to solve it. This majority consists of optimists and dreamers who believe in love and know if they keep looking, they'll find it.

Another group, fed up with the frustration, cheat. They pull the puzzle apart and reconstruct it. Come on, everybody's done it. Enter the dysfunctional soul. Desperate for companionship, they take what they can get. Thus, they fool the world with their pseudo-solution.

The third group, intellectuals, do their research. They go out and buy the book on how to solve the cube. A library full of self-help books later, they realize that they're not even one step closer to understanding love. Like the cube, love isn't something that was designed to be taught through a book. Trial-and-error is inherent in the nature of both.

The final group, myself being a charter member, are the cynics. We spend a lot of time just staring at the cube, questioning whether there's even a solution at all. We'd like to think there is, but are hesitant to spend the time to find it. What if the whole thing is just some cruel joke? We also tend to anticipate the introduction of a new puzzle every year with new colors, patterns, and rules to follow, so why bother. We become frustrated when we can't see the light at the end of the tunnel, no matter how bright that light might be. Maybe someday.

Stripped

Ego
Swaying in the Wind
Down at the Gallows
Pride
On the Chopping Block
Now Beheaded
Bullet-riddled Esteem
On the Rack
Hope lies Gutted
Faith Massacred
on the Order of
the Executioner
Your Smile
Shielded
by the Black Hood
You Wear

Stripped

6
8:00 am, Sunday morning

"Let's go back to the party," blurts Poo.

"Huh?"

"Let's go back to the club," he repeats. "It's 8 o'clock. The shit'll be rockin' by now."

"Who's spinnin' the sunrise set? Do you know?"

"Wasn't Carl Cox supposed to be there?"

"Are you shittin' me?," I ask. "No shittin' bro. Seriously."

"Why'd we ever leave in the first place then?"

"Cuz you wanted to smoke a bowl. Remember?"

"Can we get back in?"

"We can always sneak in," suggests Chad.

There's a gaping hole in the fence that encloses the back court-yard at the club.

"True."

"Yeah, let's go back to the club Dan. Just for a few hours." Jason's two cents.

"Hey, it's not my decision. It's cool with me."

As we approach the back of the club, I can tell we're in for a treat. Sometimes you can almost smell it in the air...*vibe*..a thousand joyous souls the barometer. It's electric.

I stop for a moment as we get closer, feeling a pang in my stomach as I glare at the fortress in front of us. The club is bathed in a soft white light, the aura pulsating, breathing. The whole structure is shimmering, beaming with vibe. The rest of the crew can feel it to and I can sense the urgency welling up inside each of us. Poo falls to his knees, making the sign of the cross on his chest, mesmerized by the sight.

The bass carries through the walls like a clap of thunder trailing off, leaving only the sizzling and crackling of age old karma on the wind. Looks of awe nail a face to the experience as the light begins to take shape, the sides of the aura collapsing inward, narrowing, shifting, expanding and contracting, forming, a star, now brighter than ever, leading us onward to the promised land.

"Fuck yeah," screams Poo, making a break for the hole in the fence.

The rest of us are close behind, hooting and hollering, running with a sense of purpose like none we've ever known in our adolescent lives, driven by our one true passion.

Poo destroys the hedges on the other side of the fence. A group of kids cooling down in the courtyard laugh as we pile through the hole, getting tangled in the bushes, managing to gain our composure just long enough to take a quick breather before racing for the back doors.

It's a zoo on the inside. Carl Cox is on the decks rockin' out those fuck-yeah-dance-all-night-blow-the-whole-joint-up-and-love-every-fucking-second-of-it techno jams. The shit the pros earn their keep with. Straight up, balls out, house music.

As I look around me, I smile. I don't see too much of this anymore. Miles of grinning faces. *Everyone* is dancing.

Not one person standing still. This is what it's all about.

..alive, whole, free, connected, in love once again with the flawed world around me, optimistic and empowered. If the vibe would only manifest itself physically so that others would believe and follow it's lead. Alas, it is intangible and yet reflected so magnificently in the faces of those around me.

We dance for two hours straight. Cox's mix has the momentum of a freight train. As the set starts to draw to a close, Travis stops and steps off to the side, leaning heavily on his knees. "You wanna hang in the chill out room for awhile?," I ask. Breathless, he nods his head.
"Fellas, we'll be in the back room, cool?"
"You all right?," I ask him.
"Yeah. I'm fine." But his face is flushed, like he might be dehydrated, so we stop and I buy him some juice. He drinks it down quickly and the color returns to his face.
"Thanks," he says, smiling.

There's a DJ from Los Angeles in the chill out room, goes by Curious..spinning smoothed-out, intelligent jungle. Rapid fire drum hits over dreamy, ambient terrain. For several minutes, I revel in the afterglow of Cox's set, my heart racing, beats colliding in my mind, dueling with sabers for supremacy.

As I come back around, I find my eyes drawn to Travis. He's stretched out on the floor, his shirt riding up on his hard stomach...damn, all this love in the air and I'm horny as hell. I want to touch him, not in any one place, but all over, all at once. I want to look into his eyes as he gets off. I want to...I close my eyes, fighting the fantasies, but they overtake me. I always wonder what it would be like if I ever do decide to come out to him. What will I say? What will he say? What will the circumstances be?

My fantasies swing from the totally outrageous to the sublime. The more outrageous ones typically involve me just blatantly coming on to him. We're usually in my bedroom with some jams in the background, like some of that early '96 funky ass desert trance, then the DJ cuts in some porno beats, lotsa wah-wah, then I just bust out with, "So you wanna make out or what?"

"What kinda question is that?"

"I don't know, I jus-"

"Hell yeah." So we fully start making out, grinding to the music. The more "domestic" ones usually involve a rather contrived conversation where I explain my situation to him.

"Travis, there's something I've been wanting to tell you."

"Yeah."

"I really like you."

"Cool, I like you too Dan."

"No, I mean I *really* like you."

Of course, even the mundane fantasies eventually crumble into sleazy sex.

"*Really* like you. Like a, I wanna put my tongue down your throat kind of, like you."

Man, am I queer as a football bat, or what? I open my eyes and he's rubbing his stomach, his boxers riding high, baggy jeans just barely clinging to his waist, and then I get busted checkin' him out by a guy sitting next to me. He smiles.

"The vibe is thick in here tonight, huh bro?"

"Definitely," I say, sinking back into the couch.

"It's organic almost. Like it's one of us. Dancing among us," he observes solemnly.

"Right on," I say, digging the assessment. "What's your name, bro?"

"John. Yours?"

"Danny."

Apparently, John knows about the vibe. He's a bit older, been raving since the summers of love in the late eighties. I can see it in his face, a line for every rave he's ever been to, a genuine, gentle smile, his saving grace. He sports an Irish soccer jersey, two sizes too small, brown cords and Skecher sneaks.

"Did you ever think it would come to this?," he says, looking around in wonder.

Our conversation moves quickly toward the heyday of rave culture, a topic I've never really had the opportunity to discuss with anyone before. He seems to be fairly knowledgeable, so you can imagine my ears perking up at the Gospel According to John..."I bought my first piece of wax way back in 1990. Back then, I never thought it would take off like this."

"What was the music like back then? Disco with funky beats, that kinda stuff?"

"Yeah...early house was actually a combination of the high energy disco being played in gay clubs, and the work of European artists, like Depeche Mode and Kraftwerk."

"So who brought the funk?"

"Parliament, James Brown.....house music was much more soulful back then, but colder and more electronic than the R&B that was popular at the time," he says with the authority of a scholar.

Some kids sitting next to us offer me a hit off their joint. I take a long drag as John continues his sermon. "It wasn't long before a certain synergy between English and American club culture began to thrive, them diggin' our noise, us diggin theirs..a warehouse party scene had all ready begun to develop in the U.K."

"Those were the first raves?"

"No, sometime in 1987 a couple of unrelated groups of people started throwing all-night house parties."

"In the U.K.?"

"Yeah. One crew, Psychic T.V., came from the industrial edge. Schoom was a group of South London soccer fans from the soul side of things. Their parties caught on with the trendier club kids who brought ecstasy and the love.."

"Then acid house came along, true?"

"Yeah.."

"See, I know some of my history," I affirm, smiling.

"The media blasted the culture for the negative images the term acid house produced and drove the parties underground," he says, pausing to hit the joint. "They grew in size, even though their locations were usually only available over the air waves of pirate radio stations."

"Right, I remember when all that was goin' down. I was kind of young though."

"Well, the majority of the action was in the UK still. The first summer of love in 1988, mostly illegal gatherings, occurred near the Motorway in London."

"So when did America catch on?"

"Someone started pedaling X to night clubs in Texas...and then shortly after that came the Storm Raves, with Frankie Bones and that whole crew."

"Ecstasy used to be legal?," I ask, feeling like a bit of dumb ass for not knowing better.

"Oh yeah. MDMA is a pharmaceutical drug. When the government outlawed MDMA they drove it underground. That's dollar signs to a dealer. The shit you buy out at a party like this, it's not MDMA."

"Right, I hear that a lot. Heroin and stuff."

"You'd be lucky if that's all it was. You wouldn't believe some of the crap that ends up in these pills. Especially the capsules. It's a real shame if you ask me."

"How did doctors justify prescriptions? When it was legal I mean. Depression?"

"No," he says, chuckling. "It was designed for psychotherapists to administer to their patients at sessions. It's an empathogen..the root being empathy. It was supposed to help them "open up" to their doctors and discuss their problems.

It's all about regression, tapping into the innocence we felt as children."

For some reason I find myself hanging on John's every word, like he's some sort of omnipotent being from the other side of the universe, sent to spread truth throughout the land - "If we could let go of all the baggage we carry around as adults, we would be more free to explore the true nature of ourselves. There was even the potential for applications within relationship counseling."

"How so?"

"Can you imagine the problems that a couple could solve if they shut out the world and spent an afternoon blowing up together?"

"Right."

"Ecstasy tends to allow one to speak directly from the heart."

"What if your heart is saying fuck off?," I joke. John takes the question quite seriously.

"Danny, does your heart ever really say fuck off? Or does that come from someplace else?"

"Wow, I never really thought about that."

"Most people don't. Doesn't mean you're a bad person, just means you need to start listening."

"I guess I do know what you're talking about. I call it flow though" .....I'm briefly distracted by a new DJ taking up his spot on the decks. John turns his head to see what I'm looking at. "You ever heard this guy spin?," he asks me.

"I don't know. Who is it?"

"Kid Koala. He's a madman."

"What's he spin?" My question is answered by the soothing flow of Tribe Called Quest's Q-Tip and their jam, *Award Tour*.

"Hip-hop. Right on. Does he flip a lot of wax?," I ask.

"That's an understatement."

Q-Tip's flow is interrupted by a De La Soul track. Kid cuts up the track as he lays down a jazzy breakbeat through his sampler. Then a third record comes down on the second platter. And then a fourth. A fifth.

"Skills, right?," observes John.

"Definitely." Neither of us says a word for several minutes as we gaze vacantly around the room, the gods of bass and treble tangling in the rafters above.

"Have you noticed all the bubble gummers rallyin' tonight?," he asks, pointing to a kid in the corner.

Bubble gummers are younger peeps, their backpacks typically laden with assorted trip toys, Vicks inhalers, candy and vitamins; neural first aid for the morning after. Entertaining manic sugar highs, they can be found roaming the dance floor freely, trading idyllic views on peace, love and music for pop rocks and Jolly Ranchers, dispensing hugs and swapping smiles - "Yeah, I copped a few Blo-pops on the way back in. Want one?," I ask, extending one and smiling.

"No. That shit'll rot your teeth. Thanks though."

"What's going on?," I ask, noticing a lot of the younger crew carrying clipboards around with them.

"You didn't hear? They're trying to shut the club down, city government that is. Some kids organized a petition signing."

"Really?"

"Yeah, it ended up on the agenda right after 20/20 ran that piece on rave a couple weeks ago."

"No shit. I saw that."

"People too small-minded to report on an issue objectively should stay the hell out of journalism, dontcha think?"

"Amen brother."

I remember being appalled at 20/20's dis on rave culture.

Raves. Do you know where your children are?

Raves. All night dance parties. Are your children being exposed to drugs?

"Hello...all you gotta do is fucking walk outside Barbara."

They think they've done their math.

Young people=Drugs.

Young people=Raves.

Therefore Raves=Drugs.

But all it takes is a little toying with the equation to see how backwards that logic is.   Leave raves out of it and what are you left with?   Young people and drugs looking for a new place to get high.   Leave the drugs out and what do you get?   Young people at raves.   What's wrong with that?   And are they going to show the flip side? - the sense of family that some kids find at raves, something that they don't get in their own fucking homes, the sense of community, of goodwill - hell no, that's too easy, not nearly sensationalist enough.

This is the exact reason why raves are now simply referred to as parties.   It's all about the media feeding frenzy.   Are we going to let them take the words right out of our mouths?   What are we willing to give up next?

Raves. Drugs. Children. Drugs. Techno. Drugs. If you play word association games long enough you can get people to believe whatever you want them to.   It's called brain washing.   Hell, you could probably even get somebody to believe that Hugh and Barbara are really journalists, and if you believe that, you'll believe anything —

Suddenly there's a commotion on the dance floor, peeps scattering left and right as the club fills with smoke, coughing, covering their noses with their shirts.   Tear gas. The music stops abruptly amidst jeers from the stunned crowd.

As John and I stand to see what's going on, the door to the back room flies off the hinges and crashes to the floor, a giant battering ram wielded by six men following closely behind it.   Actually they look more like stormtroopers, covered head to toe in shiny, metallic black armor.   Three of them are armed, the other three dragging a net, led by the queen muckraker herself, Barbara Walters. "There he is. That's the one," she hollers, pointing at me.

The three with the net charge, raising it high before dropping it on me.   It falls heavily over my head and I collapse. The other three head instinctively for the DJ, jostling him briefly before smashing his turntables with a large sledge-hammer and then dragging him away. I struggle briefly with the net, but it's dead weight. "Bring the boy. We'll put him with the rest."

The troopers march mechanically from the club, drag-ging me roughly behind them. The club falls away as we leave the front entrance, crumbling into pieces, the pieces swirling and dancing before getting sucked away into the great abyss. The surface we're on now is surrounded by this abyss, this blackness, this vast expanse of nothingness. I can't hear any-thing, like we're in the center of a giant vacuum, the silence as black as the surroundings...now I can hear something, but sound is moving backwards, like we're emerging from the vacuum. It sounds like a large crowd of people, screaming and taunting. I smell smoke, but it doesn't smell like wood burning..smells like, well, kind of like plastic. Son of a bitch. They're burning records. It's a witch hunt.

The world into which I'm propelled is straight out of *Fahrenheit 451*. Still tangled in the net, it's difficult to get a good look around, but I'm reminded of my visit to Times Square when I was a kid - lots of tall buildings with large movie screens mounted on them stand to either side of me, vehicles for the media's propaganda. Rave. Drugs. Techno. Drugs. The images flash intermittently on the giant screens, the reddish rotation of sirens reflecting off the mist.

One of the soldiers, his chest adorned with medals for courageous acts of censorship, stands precariously on a make-shift stage with a megaphone carrying on about dancing and the evils of the world. It's like Footloose meets Star Wars. Positively bizarre.

Hundreds more of the trooper-like soldiers stand in the street tossing records into barrels harboring blazing fires. There's a cage up ahead with about 50 or so kids locked up inside. Their mouths have been taped shut and their arms and legs tied. It looks like that's where they're taking me.

"Let's see what he's all about first," threatens Barbara, ordering the troopers to stop.

I'm removed from the net and shoved directly into a rotting wooden chair about ten feet from the bars of the cage. My hands are shackled to the arms, my feet to the legs and a device placed on my head. A tingle races from the silvery electrodes on my head all the way down to my feet as the screens and lights nearby shut down, all the electricity in the vicinity racing through my body.

The next sensation is unexplainable, like tiny feelers on the surface of my brain. It almost tickles. A bad tickle though. It's probing, scanning. Like the ultimate invasion of privacy, it's attempting to read my thoughts, back and forth, hesitating momentarily as if encountering something interesting and then continuing, prying, and then suddenly the screens flicker back to life and it's Dan T.V.

Motherfuckers are broadcasting my thoughts!

And my fantasies. A multimedia extravaganza of adolescent lust. Travis. My buddy Keith. Tony, my old neighbor.

"Aaah, he's a faggot too," curdles Barbara. "You know what we do to faggots."

Ten soldiers appear from around the corner of a building dragging a massive chain of ass beads across the ground. At this point I'm screaming bloody murder. Dream or no dream, thousand pound ass beads are not cute.

"What'd ya thinka that faggot?," barks Barbara furiously.

Then the sky opens up. For a moment, time stands still. Then comes the music. Like a direct feed from another planet, the dirtiest, meanest, nastiest, funkiest synth my ears have ever beheld. The kind of jam God would spin. Interplanetary house *muzak*.

Descending straight from the heavens come the DJs, all wearing campy superheroes costumes. Sasha. Keoki. Carl

Cox. Paul Oakenfold. Frankie Knuckles. Josh Wink. Doc Martin. The hometown heroes, D-Extreme, Chris Fortier, Andy Hughes, Sandy and Kimball Collins. One right after the other, they ride the lightning down.

Moby even showed up. He's got a turntable strapped to his back, chucking records at the troopers, the rest of the guys firing brilliant blue laser beams from their eyes, channeling the music.

Most of the soldiers are on their knees now, their hands clawing at their ears. Like a scene from *Scanners*, their heads erupt from their shoulders as the bass lands all around them, their bodies exploding as the beams slice through the air.

The peeps in the cage have broken free and armed themselves with dance in an attempt to restore the vibe. In seconds, vibe is rocketing from their fingertips disintegrating all the troopers in it's path and putting Barbara on the run.

Keoki spies her out of the corner of his eye and walks calmly over to Moby to borrow a twelve inch.
"20/20 my ass. Try legally fucking blind, bitch," he spits, hurling a record and severing her head, obscenities still flying from her mouth.

My brain logs a freeze frame of Keoki offing Barb and it melts colorfully into my subconscious like the last frame of a comic book..

Building Fences

No white picket
pseudo American Dream
Barbed wire Concrete and steel
Your scheme
Fraught with cynicism
and distrust
The means to an end
or the end of the means
Fuck you and your
self righteous brigade
My tirade has just begun
yet you pay no mind
You go right on...
Building Fences
Are you shutting me out
or shutting yourself in
You can't win
when you are
your own worst enemy
Self-important nobody
Can't you see
I'm not about to flee
Judgment calls
you put up walls
and go right on...
Building Fences

Your fantasy world's
a fucking joke
Stoke the embers
if you feel the need
but know that I am here
Gaining speed
on your pitiful game
No one to blame
but yourself
You had to have your two cents
Now I'm ripping down
Your fucking fence

7

Deter Barnes. Deter's not your typical skate punk. I occasionally catch him listening to classic rock; Jethro Tull, Santana, Zeppelin and Pink Floyd are his favorites, depending on his mood, maybe even some Steve Miller. Of course, he also listens to a lot of the bands that the rest of the skate rats listen to, but that's besides the point. He doesn't always dress like a skater either, known to skate in a shirt and a tie just to draw attention and get a laugh. I even saw him compete one time in a purple tutu to Beethoven's Fifth.

Deter's also smart as a whip. Not that most skaters are dumb, but Deter was in the top five of his graduating class in high school. I have to respect him for that. Anybody that can smoke as much dope as he did in high school, and still keep up, more power to them. As I look over at him, I can't help but think about how cute he is too.

An old, tattered Beastie Boys T-shirt hangs loosely on his wiry frame. His shorts sag, hanging down to around his calves and his Airwalk kicks, a tattoo of Scooby-Doo with a hit of acid on his tongue barely visible on his ankle. Classic. His hair is a sandy brown bob. It falls in his face a lot, but it never phases him. He's got a really infectious Jeff Spicolli stoner laugh too. You can't help but love the kid.

"Wow D, you look like you had a rough night kid," he observes from the couch where he sits packing his Graffix. "You still doin' that ravin' thing?," with more than a hint of disdain.

"Yeah, I just dropped the rest of the boys off."

"Oh yeah, you went ravin' and you didn't bring me any candy Dan?," he asks sarcastically.

"How was it? Big Flop, that is, I mean, uh, Big Top?"

"Pretty phat I guess. Same old shit, you know."

"Ravin' is for pussies and leprechauns Dan, you haven't heard?"

For someone whose tastes seem to be so eclectic, Deter clearly has a thing against house music. Maybe it's that skater vs. raver dynamic. Deter seems like the type to be bigger than that though. I suppose I might give him too much credit.

"I don't know what you've heard, but I go for the music, bro."

"I can't wait 'til rave culture goes mainstream. I'd like to see how you feel then. All the pussies and leprechauns gettin' down on Club MTV. WannaBe Productions and their record release parties at Walmart. Rave themed birthday parties for nine year olds, whistles, blow pops and Dr. Suess hats for everybody, pin the tail on the junkie, playing musical chairs to DJ Tired's mad mix of old school classics, ecstasy in the cake mix-,"

"It won't matter bro. Those who know what's up will just take it to the next level. It's all part of the plan."

"Oh yeah, which plan is that? World domination?," he scoffs.

"It's evolution bro. We're a civilized society, true?"

"Arguable. Some would say we're devolving as a society."

"Bingo. The world around us is evolving, but as human beings were devolving, as you say."

"Your point?," he asks snidely.

"My point is that rave culture, like any microcosmic, utopian model for society, is about the evolution of thought and behavior-"

"Dan, can you even spell *microcosmic*?," he asks cynically.

"A way to rekindle the intimate fires of the human race," I continue, inspired by my conversation with John earlier.

"Ew, sounds romantic."

"It's all mutating right now Detes, the roots burying themselves deep in the collective consciousness, taking hold, festering like a virus, waiting for just the right moment to strike. Soon you'll be one of *us*," I say dramatically.

"Well *we*, are on to you freaks."

"There's always someplace to hide when you're underground," I challenge playfully.

"Yeah, well worms think they're pretty underground too," Deter says, laughing to himself.

I decide to cut right to the chase in a deliberate attempt to avoid spending the rest of the night, glued to his couch, defending myself. "You got any of that kind left bro? Like a gram to be exact."

"I don't think I have that much left dude," he says, shaking his head

"Can you check?"

"Sure, just let Uncle Detes treat ya to a couple bong swats first."

This happens every time I buy from Deter. He insists on getting me high as a kite before selling me any dope. Normally I wouldn't complain, quite the contrary, but tonight is different. I'm exhausted.

"One swat Detes. I can't stay. My brain hurts from last night."

"Ah-hah..thats my boy. And then one more, right? And then 6 for the road."

He laughs. I cringe. I know he's right.

"I was just about to put in the trilogy. You gotta hang out.

Besides, you're leaving next week. Stay for Yoda, if not for me."

"I can't stay bro," I insist with a smile.

"Luke needs your help in the Dagobah system," he mimics in his best Yoda voice.

I grin and shake my head. As I light the bowl, I notice the gnarly red hairs in the skunky bud. The kindest of kind. Magically delicious, as Deter would say.

He constantly makes television and film references when he gets stoned - sometimes obscure, but always amusing. Aside from being a huge Star Wars fan, he is also heavily into 70's copper flicks and a huge cartoon freak. Except for Scooby-Doo, he's not really into the more popular cartoons, though. No Tom and Jerry. No Looney Tunes. He digs hard on the old, tripped out Spiderman, the Super Friends with the Legion of Doom, G-Force, Robotech, GI Joe, Dungeons and Dragons, Transformers..80's toons like we used to watch on Saturday mornings and after school as kids.

"That's a one hitter D. Finish that," he says condescendingly as I try to pass him the bong.

He always gets me with that one. Five "one-hits" later, I'm always out of my head.

"As my friends the Keebler elves would say....uncommonly good," he jokes as I finish the bowl.

I'm stoned. The cantina scene from the original *Star Wars* is on the tube. It sparks Deter's imagination and he rewinds our conversation to evolution and starts to tell me his theory about aliens...the black sheep of Darwinism. I've heard it before, but I indulge him anyway.

"You always hear these freaks on TV talkin' about gettin' abducted and shit. And what do they all say? Aliens got like really plain features and big heads and shit right? Like this freak right here—" He points to the alien in the cantina with the oblong head and the bug eyes to illustrate his point. "See, all he needs is his brain dude. Look at him. He's just chillin' with that big old brain. Pure intelligence. He doesn't need anything else. It's evolution bro. Like the caveman. He didn't need all that hair anymore, just like we don't need anything but this anymore," he whispers, tapping his finger on the side of his head.

My head feels like it's full of lead. It takes every ounce of concentration I can muster to look Deter in the eyes and hear him out. Did I also mention that Deter loves to talk when he's stoned?

"Evolution is occurring simultaneously in different dimensions D. That's where the sightings come in. The aliens have found a way to travel between dimensions—," he says, pausing for dramatic effect, "or down the evolutionary chain, however you wanna look at it. Time has no meaning. Everything's happening all at once. The guy who invented the clock was an idiot," he cries maniacally.

"You want somethin' to drink D? You're lookin' a little white in the face."

"Yeah dude," I somehow manage to vocalize. "Water's cool."

Deter gets up and goes to his kitchen to get me a glass of water. I decide it's about a good a time as any to start motivating home, so I follow him. As he opens the fridge, I go in for the kill. "Can you check on that bud? I need to be headin' home."

"Yeah. Here-," he says, handing me the glass of water. "I'll be down in a sec," and then he runs upstairs to weigh out a sack for me.

As I stand alone in the dark kitchen, I start to think about tonight. Me and the guys had planned on going to a party on the other side of town. Some guy that buys from Chad is supposed to have a couple DJs come out and spin some records. I'm sure there will be pills available, but eating a pill tonight isn't an option for me - I *have to* start packing tomorrow. It's going to be a long week, no rest for the wicked.

Deter interrupts my train of thought, bouncing down

the stairs with a bud in his hand.

"This is all I got kid," he says, handing me enough green to roll a joint.

"No shit?"

"Sorry, but you have to give me more notice Dan. I don't keep quantity around my pad anymore. It's too risky."

"I told the guys this would happen."

"Oh, you're buying for the whole crew?"

"Fuck that, it's every man for himself now."

"Stay and smoke one more bowl with me and you'll be set for awhile."

"No bro, I app.."

"Dan, I never see your ass anymore and you're leaving me next week. Two more bong swats for me, word?," he says, leading me back into the living room.

"Yeah, yeah, yeah."

"I can't believe I just said that."

"What?"

"*Word.* I think your boy Jason is wearin' off on me. That kid's got me hooked on ebonics. I asked my buddy Ryan the other day, 'Yo, what up homes?' I never used to talk that b-boy crap before. Now I'm like Deter Barnes, the Original Gangsta, droppin' science on your ass, *biatch.*"

"Yeah, he's got me talkin' like that too."

"But you're into that stuff Dan. I hate that shit. Don't get me wrong. It's not a white versus black thing, it's kind of a shit talkin' thing, know what I'm saying? Look at Tupac. I mean, how am I supposed to sympathize with him and other victims of inner city violence when they're out there glorifying it all the time? You live by the sword, you die by the sword."

A conversation with Deter can swing within moments from cartoons and skating to the extinction of the rain forests and the plight of third world countries. It's a function of his intelligence and the fact that he's very opinionated. I don't mind. I enjoy the long lost art of conversation.

"Playing devil's advocate, there are people in the inner city that *don't* support people like Tupac and what he stood for."
"They're a minority Dan. A silent minority at that."
"So what do you suggest be done about it?"
"I don't know. I'm starting to adopt a rather nihilistic attitude towards it all. I say let the inner city self destruct. It'll make a hell of a skate park after the cease fire. I'll be out there poppin' ollies off the bodies in the street. Fuck it." Seconds later, his head is already somewhere else. "I didn't tell ya did I bro?," he asks, rummaging through some videotapes on the floor.
"What's that?"
"I scored all the old school Scoobies on tape," popping one in the VCR.
"Oh yeah."
"Yeah, back when they had guest stars every week. The Harlem Globetrotters. Sonny and Cher. The Three Stooges. Remember that shit?"

All potheads like to think that they are part of some twisted herb-smoking order. That's where the crew came up with the concept of F.O.G., Friends of the Ganja. In a sense, it justifies the vice. We like to think that everyone in the world that is down, certainly must smoke dope. I'm sure there's even someone out there who swears up and down that Jesus was a stoner and has pictures to prove it. With Deter's affinity for his boy Scooby, he feels that surely Scooby is one of *us*.
"You know how I know?"
"How's that?"
"Scooby *and* Shag exhibit all the tell-tale signs," he states emphatically. "I mean, they're always hungry."
"Right."
"They seem to be the only ones that see the ghosts. You never see Fred or Daphne or Thelma trippin' like that, right?"
"True."
"They cruise around in the back of the 'Mystery Machine'

with all those trippy designs painted on it just smokin' down like fiends, I'm telling you man. And just look at Shaggy..that kid just looks like a stoner," he says, pointing at the TV.

"Ya know, it's no wonder to me that we'll go down in history as the hallucination generation. The *great space coaster,* dude..what the fuck is that!? Have you ever thought about it?"

"Not lately-"

*"The new zoo revue--*remember that one? And don't even get me started on Sesame Street. It's all that 70's and early 80's television that left us so thirsty for psychedelia. "

"Fraggle Rock-," I think nostalgically to myself.

"Yeah..*crack* rock is what I'm sayin'. The Dozers were movin' mad amounts of the shit from that meth lab under the garden."

I always seem to leave Deter's apartment looking at life in just a slightly different way than ever before.

"I hate to leave, but I really ought to," I say, standing up to get my wallet.

"No charge Dan. Look at it as a little going away present."

"No shit bro? Thanks...you're the man. Am I gonna see you before I leave?"

"Definitely dude. I'll get with ya before Friday," he assures me.

"Cool," I say, hugging him on the way out. "Take care," I add. He smiles and closes the door behind me.

As I fumble for my keys in my pocket, relief creeps into my tired bones. Nothing else stands between me and my bed. Well, almost nothing. Just the open road and my mom. Better stop and get some Visine on the way home. Maybe she'll be out playing cards with her friends. After all, it is a Saturday night. Then again, she sometimes invites her friends over to our place to play cards. Too high to care, I get in my car and head home.

8

My mom and I live in a small, rented two bedroom house next to a private college on the north side of town. Her car isn't in the driveway when I pull up and it's a good thing since I'm no less stoned than when I left Deter's, and I completely spaced on the Visine. I make a mental note to thank her for the tuna casserole that she left in the fridge for me. There's a message on the answering machine. It's Jason.

"This is your official wake up call, Danny. If we don't hear back from you at my place in the next half-hour or so, we're coming over and dragging you out of bed. You've been warned. Oh, this is J by the way...oh and we got mad pills for tonight. Hope you're down. Peace."

Shit. There goes my sleep. No..I have to sleep. Maybe I'll lock all the doors and windows, so they can't get in. No..they'll find a way in. I could park my car down the street and around the corner, and they'd never know I was home. No..they'd break in to wait for me. None of them has any respect for my mom's place. I'll just skip the nap, take my own car tonight and leave early. They might go for that. It's worth a shot.

I fire up the coffee-maker and make myself a cup. Sipping it slowly at the kitchen table, I read the note my mom left for me. She did go to play cards. The note also mentions the leftovers in the fridge and that she'll be home late. Love, mom.

The sliding glass door in the living room slides open loudly. It's the crew, rested and ready to do it all again. "Oh, Danny boy, the pipe is calling," bellows Poo, dancing around the living room with a freshly packed bowl in his hand.

I ignore them at first in an attempt to let them know what kind of mood I'm in. Then I look up. "Sup fellas?"

"Get my message kid?," asks Jason, patting me on the back.

"Danny, you score any bud?," via Travis.

"You got anything to eat bro?," via Chad, as he opens up the fridge to look for himself.

"Swat?," via Poo, who offers me the pipe.

"Yes, kind of, no, and what the fuck do you think you're doing smokin' in my house?," I snarl.

"Wow, cranky aren't we Danny. Did we not get our nap?"

I get up and walk over to Chad, closing the fridge. He fixes a betrayed stare on me as the rest of the guys take over the living room, turn on the TV and continue smoking.

"If you guys are gonna do that, at least open the frickin' back door," I holler from the kitchen. "This ain't the crack house," I explain to Chad.

"I know, I know. It ain't the soup kitchen either, right?"

"You got that right."

"So you 'kind of' scored some buds? How does that work?"

"All I got was a little nug. Deter was out."

I let the guys know that I have to shower and change clothes before we leave. They're only half listening, as they have found the treasured *Ren and Stimpy* tape, popped it in the VCR and are thoroughly engrossed.

The shower is almost religious. I've been in the same sweat-soaked rags from the night before, all day long. A shower is usually the only place I get any peace on any given day. It's also usually the only opportunity I get to whack off. I'm a strong believer in self-gratification. Nothing wrong with tossin' a wad in the shower once in a while. Hmm...I wonder if that's why my vision's so shitty? Maybe I'm going blind. Well, at least I'll be happy, healthy and blind. With AIDS running rampant, you'd think doctors would start prescribing it. Jerk off twice and call me in the morning. Not a bad deal if you ask me.

My thoughts are interrupted by a loud banging on the door. "Hurry up D," echoes Jason's voice through the door. "Kid's spinning around 9." Scott is a DJ friend of ours. Going by Kid Dynamite, he spins mostly old school breaks and hip-hop.

I jump out of the shower, throw a towel around myself and run to my room to put on some clothes. Moments later, Trav appears at my bedroom door. I turn around just in time to catch him gazing at my bare ass.

"Hey," he says, grinning ear to ear. "It can wait."

"No, it's cool bro. Come on in," I say, blushing, pulling up my underwear.

"I'll wait," he repeats, embarrassed.

I can't help but smile as I finish getting dressed and return to the kitchen. Things are definitely going to get interesting when Travis and I go away together. I'm really looking forward to getting away from here; from the drugs and the long nights.

"Ready to do this?," asks Poo, handing me the last of my coffee.

"Yup," I nod.

Chad, Trav and Jason file into the kitchen, as we prepare to leave. To my dismay, they actually bothered to turn off the TV and VCR and shut the back door. Probably Trav's work. "I'm taking my own car fellas. I can't stay all night. I hung out at Deter's all afternoon and never got any sleep."

"Doh," chokes Jason, covering his mouth with his hand. Poo and Chad smile at each other, as Jason heads for the front door. "What's up?," I ask.

"Nothin' dude," replies Chad.

"We might as well go together. You're not going to be able to sleep anytime soon," says Trav, shaking his head.

As I drink the last drop of my coffee, I notice it tastes particularly bad. Trav nods his head apologetically. Bastards put a pill in my coffee. Uncool. I stand staring at Jason for a minute. A cold, hard stare. "Paybacks are hell Jas. Ya little shit."

"I'll look forward to it. You can hook me up anytime, Dan."

"Let's go bro. What's done is done. Might as well enjoy it," encourages Trav.

"We're still taking my car," I say, motioning toward the door. No dissenters.

"We gotta stop and get some buds," calls Jason from the back seat as we climb into my ride.

"Where?," I ask, lifting my eyes to the rearview mirror.

"My boy Lazarus can hook us up."

"Lazarus?"

"Yeah, Chad knows him."

"Laz is my coke connection," admits Chad hesitantly. "It's up to you guys. Laz is shady as hell, but he could definitely hook us up."

"How shady?"

"I don't think the brother's seen the sun in years."

"Where's he live?"

"The Bends," a series of narrow, curvy, residential roads on the far side of town, populated by crack dealers and assorted other scurvy; a nigtmarish landscape painted with toothless meth peddlers on bicycles, kids playing kickball in the street at all hours of the night, and homes in varying stages of depreciation.

"Whatever," I say, turning on the radio.

"Atta boy," says Jason, slapping me on the shoulder.

Travis gazes at me apprehensively as I start the car. We arrive in Hades no more than a half hour later. "It's right up here on the left bro," instructs Chad.

"Which one?"

"Just park right here on the street. This is cool."

I can hear Biggie Small's "Things Done Changed" shaking the foundation of the dilapidated house as we innocently approach, crossing the barren yard. Poo trips on the skeletal remains of a bicycle buried in the dirt.

"Ow, fuckin-a," he yelps, grabbing his ankle.

"You all right?," I ask, giggling childishly.

"Yeah, I'll live," he replies as Jason pounds on the front door.

The volume on the tunes drops a notch and the door is answered shortly afterwards. Meet Laz. Blunted eyes, dark brown skin and a neo-prehistoric Shaft afro to die for. 110% street dealer and proud of it.

"What up, yo?," he asks Chad, opening the door and reclaiming his seat on the sectional.

The house is sparsely "decorated." A large, filthy pit group for negotiations is the centerpiece. Laz is on the phone, a cordless cradled between his ear and shoulder.

*I've been robbin motherfuckers since the slave ships, with the same clip, and the same .45, two point blank, a motherucker sure to die..*chants Biggie from the grave.

Laz aims the remote lazily at the stereo and the carousel spins noisily, Mobb Deep taking the stage..*I got you stuck off the realness, we be the infamous, you heard of us, official Queens Bridge murderers, the Mobb comes equipped for warfare, beware-*

"I'll freeze a motherfucker down like Hans Solo," Laz snarls into the phone, feeding on the drama of the verse..*ain't no such things as halfway crooks..*

"Yeah, well Luke Skywalker betta pull up some sky cuz I'ma toss his ass off a bridge, faggot ass bitch."

Ever met somebody that fit a stereotype so well that you feel like you're on the set of a movie? Like they can't possibly be for real? I feel like I've landed the starring role in the latest Wu Tang video. It's an act, it has to be - there's nobody on the other end of that line - "Shit nigga, I move more ice than Dorothy fuckin' Hammill, who you think you're talkin' to?" This can't be happening. I think it's time to excuse myself, splash some water and let Chad handle this. "Bathroom?," I ask Chad, standing up.

"Yeah dog, it's in the back," Laz says, cupping his hand over the phone. "Stay away from the tub, fools be comin' over all the time gettin' stupid high, some motherfucker took a shit in my tub."

"No shit."

"For real shit, drunk on 40's, blunted as a muhfucker, took a dump in my tub, no lie. I'm leavin' it 'til I find the faggot that did it, so I can stick his face in it, then I'ma put my nine to his head and make 'em eat it. All of it," he says, adjusting the pick in his afro and returning to his conversation.

"It can wait," I decide, sitting back down.

Speaking of nines, there's a gun on the end table. It must be a prop. This isn't reality, it can't be. People can't possibly live like this. It's like a sinister, urbanesque Candid Camera - Laz is going to pick up the gun, put it to my temple and squirt water in my eye, enter Alan Funt stage left, no, a flag pops out, it says "Bang! You're dead", Laz laughs maniacally and Fanny Flagg comes toppling out of the closet..

"Dude, what the fuck? Is this guy for real?," I whisper in Chad's ear.

"Chill Dan. We'll be outta here in five."

Another brother enters from stage right, emerging from a bedroom followed closely by a thick cloud of smoke. "Got half a z, yo, straight?"

"How much?"

"Fitty."

"Yeah, that's straight," agrees Chad.

"Word, pay Laz."

He throws a half ounce of buds in Chad's lap and returns to the bedroom, staring Jason down in the corner. Chad places a ten and two twenties on the table.

"Peace out ya'll," says Laz, slapping Chad's hand in goodwill.

We mumble a round of casual laters, peaces and see yas on the way out the door.

I start the car quickly and uncharacteristically don my seatbelt, jerking the wheel and darting into the street. No one says a word for several minutes.

"Jason, you're full of brilliant ideas, arentcha?"

"Hey, Laz has love for-"

"Yeah, loads of love. You guys are best buds, I can tell."

"He's Chad's boy, I-"

"*I move more ice than Dorothy fuckin' Hamill*," I say, brutishly mimicking Laz.

"So he talks a lotta shit."

"*Faggot ass bitch*," I continue.

"Dan, you and your dimestore conscience. Get over it."

I slam on the brakes and the guys lurch forward in their seats.

"Get out."

"What?"

"I said get out."

Jason yanks the handle and throws the door open angrily, stepping out into the street and slamming it closed loudly. I put the accelerator to the floor and pin the tires to the gravel on the next turn.

"What the fuck is that supposed to mean? Dimestore conscience?"

"I don't know but you can't just leave him there," insists Poo, turning and looking through the back window.

"I'm just driving around the block. He'll be fine."

"Why you freakin, bro?," Chad asks me from the passenger seat.

"I can't stand it when he runs his mouth like that."

"So you get all self-righteous."

"Looks like somebody's playing God again," Poo says under his breath.

I'm not being self-righteous. Am I? The tone of the voice in my head frightens me. Maybe I am. No, I'm personalizing, though I dare not say anything. They're my friends though. Shit, I *am* freakin'. "I'm not playing God," I say as calmly as possible.

The next turn takes me down a particularly dark street. All the street lamps have been disemboweled, like someone had taken pot shots at them, used them for target practice.

"This isn't the kind of neighborhood you ought to be playing games in," says Poo sternly.

"No shit. You think I want to be here?," I remind him.

"Well, let's go then."

"Where'd he go?," rolling my window down.

A dark figure emerges from the bushes on the curb, bolting into the street and up to the car. I swerve and brake, and the next thing I know, there is a hand around my throat, a deep voice barking commands.

"Get out of the car motherfucker."

I struggle to get a better look, but the figure's face is concealed by the roof of the car, the hand holding me firmly in my seat. Travis starts to get out..

"Put it in park and get out motherfucker." The hand is tight around my neck, and I reach down to take the car out of gear.

"I said get out of the car..faggot," and the figure bends and pokes his hooded head through the window. It's Jason.

"You son of a bitch," I shout, clutching my heart. Poo knew all along and now he's in stitches. "That is so uncool."

"And kickin' your boy out of your car is?," he asks, climbing into the backseat.

I look at Travis and he shrugs as if to say, "The kid's got a point."

"Whatever dude."

"Yep. That's what I thought. Now make like I'm Miss Daisy and drive, *biatch*."

9
9:00 pm, Sunday night

The party is hyped even though it's early, the smell of smoked meat lingering in the air alongside the aroma of good smoke. There's a keg flowing in the garage. Not too many people here yet; probably about 15 heads including us, if that. Kid D is spinning some records in the living room. As I approach him, he looks up from the turntables and drops his headphones off his ears.

"What up dude?," he asks, extending his hand with a smile.

"Nada bro," I reply, returning his love fist to fist.

Scotty's a cultural mutt, one of those kids that's never been quite sure where he fits in, or if he wants to fit in at all. It's unfortunate, but at our age there's a certain amount of pressure to establish some parameters for one's self so our peers can file us away and attach a gig with a face.

He's wearing a Quicksilver hat, a souvenir from his surfing days, pulled down low over his eyes, a t-shirt endorsing Technics 1200 turntables, and a pair of baggy skate shop cords that swallow up his bare feet, compliments of his earthy side which he discovered touring with Phish. Scott's mother is Hispanic-American, his father a light skinned black man from the Caribbean, and there's a certain offbeat charm in the eclectic cross section of ethnicities and subcultures he represents.

"How you been?," I ask.

"Just kickin' it bro. You know me. Long as I got my jams to keep me company, I don't need much else. You're leavin' next week, huh? Big college boy?"

"You know it. Friday. I can't wait. Way things have been, I wouldn't survive another summer around here."

"Oh yeah? You been blowin' up a lot? Partyin' hard?," with an evil grin, turning to look at the television behind him - Colecovision, a couple of peeps are jacked in playing Donkey Kong, an audio feed to his mixer. He cocks his head and grins, turning a pot to the right, the theme song coming up slowly in the speakers around the room.

"Only you Scotty," I say smiling.

"Old school like Tang brother," he says slapping my palm.

"So what's up? You know you still haven't hooked me up with a copy of that tape yet" - Scott spent the better part of the winter taking a series of classes in audio engineering. The lesson that excited him most dealt with sound frequencies in which his instructor explained to the class that certain frequencies are inaudible to the human ear, the higher ones capable of driving a person insane and the lower ones, of affecting one's inner workings, if you know what I mean. It inspired him to produce the quintessential bass tape, load it with low frequency waves and title it "Incontinent Beats: Bass to Make Your Bowels Move." It didn't put me on the shitter, but it definitely rocks. I'm a sucker for a phat bass line..the rhythm..the rebel.

"Oh...I'm glad you reminded me. You know I'm almost done with my volume two."

"Oh yeah.."

"It's called 'Ground Effects'..all low rider bass."

"You put that old MC ADE track on there?"

"Yeah bro. It's hella cool. Mad old school...the shit makes you wanna roll up your sleeves and peg your Z Caviariccis. DJ Magic Mike....classic Two Live Crew...."

"Mix-alot?"

"Me and Kid Sensation, home away from home, with the black Bens limo and the cellular phone," he recites in a nasal voice. *My posse's on Broadway. My posse's on Broadway.*

"No shit. You took it way back."

"Then I drop in *New York, New York*..that old techno track, cut it up real nice.....and almost the whole second side is the original Jam Pony Express shit."

"Right on."

"So you liked the first one then? Funky like that monkey on your back?"

"Funkier bro."

"I gotta copy for ya in my car. I've been so busy, I-"

"No sweat. I understand."

"Yeah, it's just that I've been trying to line up some gigs up for myself and I haven't had much time."

"Any luck?"

"Yeah, I'm going to be spinning at the grand opening of that new club down on Mercy Drive. You heard about it? The Factory?"

"No. Did you say Mercy?"

"Yeah, I know. Shady part of town right? Don't look at me. Rent's cheap I guess, and besides, they know that word of mouth can pack the place no matter where they locate. It's a no brainer anymore. Build it and they will come," he adds dramatically.

"Who's headlining? Do you know?"

"I don't know if they figured that out yet. There was talk about bringing in a few west coast DJs. Kind of an east meets west type of thing. Trance was mentioned, the Hardkiss brothers...umm..DJ Dan. Efex and Tron from Chicago were also contacted I think."

"No shit. That's a phat bill."

"Well, that's their wish list, they haven't settled on anything yet. They won't land all those names, but they need to get it straightened out so I can start promoting. I told them I would help if they would get me the info."

"That's straight. You gettin' paid?"

"Fuck no dude. It's all pro boner," he jokes, feigning with his hand like he's jerking off.

"Gotta start somewhere kid."

"Yeah, I thought the skills were 'sposed to pay the bills though...can't figure out why everybody's sweatin' the technique. Check it bro," he insists, lifting his headphones back to his ears and cutting in his bomb track. It's the gem of his collection. Every DJ has one, that record that no one else can track down.

His fingers work the vinyl back and forth as cheers of excitement go up from the small crowd dancing in the living room, the bass rolling across the floor and washing over them.

I can feel the ecstasy taking over, palms sweating, a little claustrophobic, and the room suddenly seems smaller. The breeze coming through the back screen door seems inviting, so I step outside for a breath of fresh air.

Standing next to the gate in the side yard is a group of young girls smoking a joint, their high pitched voices accompanied by a set of wind chimes singing over my head. An ecstasy wave rocks my body and I smile, tilt my head back and close my eyes, the drama of the evening quickly forgotten.

Maybe this pill wasn't such a bad idea after all. Ecstasy makes me feel inspired, glad to be alive, a master of the possibilities, rather than a slave to doubt. Danny Boyle, Toxic Cowboy.

The forces of good have become adept at exposing the

emotional scam artists sent by the opposition, but their propaganda is strong and not easily discredited.

One of the girls approaches me slowly, like 'I know you, psych, no I don't, O.K., maybe' - "Danny Boyle, is that you?," and as she gets closer, I recognize her as an old friend. Kind of. I call them "chemical friends," people who I only have one thing in common with..ecstasy. I can't remember her name.

"Hey girl," I respond, hugging her tightly as she rushes up to me. "What's goin' on?"

"Nothing. Long time, no see."

"Yeah, right. What have you been up to?"

"Blowin' up," she says, giggling, rubbing my arm and grinding her teeth.

"Really? I thought you had enough, we're tryin' to clean up."

"Yeah, I was," she answers, kneading the skin on my arm with her fingers, "but this guy I've been dating has been giving me free pills. He deals and stuff, so you know.."

The kiss of death, befriending or dating someone that deals ecstasy; hard to say no when the pills are free. It's a difficult thing to admit to myself, but I'd be a mess in that kind of situation. All that stands between myself and a serious habit is cash flow - X is just too damn expensive.

"It's the season too. School's out, summer's here, you know me Dan."

No, I really don't - chemical ties..remembering a party back when downers were the bomb, valium, ludes, whatever, and the Junior class would get drunk and do them all night, get sloppy as hell and love every second of it. Enter the social holocaust; never mind that no one ever remembered them, there was always pictures. Girlfriend fell flat on her face outside on the concrete and split her face from her lip up to her nose. Even in the dim light of the backyard, I can still see the scar.

"You wanna come meet my friends, help us smoke this joint?"
"Actually I'd love to, but I kind of have to go to the bathroom," I admit, only half-lying.
"Oh, well it was good seeing you. We'll be here late, so maybe later," she says, hugging me again. "Right on. Take care O.K."

She smiles longingly, walking back to her friends and waving shyly as I wave back and walk inside. The party has filled out a bit...deal going down in the corner, roll of twenties and a ten pack of pills, as Kid works the crowd, headed for trancey outer-space. When it feels right, he'll bring everybody back to earth with a perfectly timed breakbeat. I'm hoping he brought some of his old school rap vinyl with him...Eric B. and Rakim, EPMD, Too Short, Boogie Down Productions, "Yo Scotty, lay your hands on me brother."

Moments later he's yanking records left and right out of his stash. Everybody's a DJ these days, but few remember where it all started. Nobody can ride a fader and cut like a hip-hop DJ. Today, you don't even really need skills. All you need is a good record collection. Fortunately, Scott has both. "Scotty," I holler over the music, "and a side order of jungle please. To go."

The jungle track starts slow, but builds quickly. Then Scott drops the bombs, one after the other, bass dropping like dominoes. P.E.'s "Bring the Noise." Marley Marl's "Symphony." KRS-One. Ice-T. Grandmaster Flash's "The Message." Fuck yeah. Jungle and hip-hop is *the* sound.

Beats are like a sonic blueprint, a rhythmic connect-the-dots, the building blocks of the groove. Jungle beats are fast. Hip-hop beats are slow. A rather chaotic arrangement, yet hip-hop brings method to the madness that is jungle.

I remember Scotty told me once that all Elvis really needed was a phat 808 drum break and he could have ruled the world...visions of Elvis, sitting in a rocking chair on a porch somewhere in the midwest, nodding his head to N.W.A, and I smile.

    As Scott gets ready to take a break, he looks at me, snatches the last record off the turntable and holds it against his head. "Ear wax bro." He tugs on his ear. "Ear." He holds up the record. "Wax. Get it. Ear. Wax. Forget it."

    I smile and shake my head. Poo and Jason emerge from the garage with beers in their hands. Travis is not far behind.

"Where's Chad?," I ask.

"Where do you think?"

"Gettin' rid of the rest of those doses?," but I know the answer.

"Scotty, you gotta mic handy?," asks Jason.

"Yeah bro, you wanna drop some shit?"

"Was thinkin' about it."

    Jason's drunk. When he gets drunk his tongue gets loose and he can flow like a madman. Scotty loops a beat for him while he unravels the cord on the microphone.

"This is for my boy Danny, my boys Chad, Poo and Travis."

Some from the old school might call us suckas
Stay the hell of the crack you fader ridin' muthafuckas
Cuz this ain't the old school, not even the new school
This jam is original, yeah this is our own school
A school where MCs get jacked like a vette
You think I'm talkin' shit kid, I ain't through yet
This jam's a dissertation on the hip hop scene
It's all about the beats, it's all about the green
We came to get down, but we ain't jumpin' around
My boy Scott's on the cut, check out the new hyped sound..

    Scott proceeds to effortlessly cut and scratch his way right into a Slick Rick joint as the few gathered in the living room give Jason a round of applause.

"Yeah?," he asks me, stepping down and grabbing his beer off the speaker.

"Encore. Encore," shouts Poo.

Jason now has the undivided attention of the majority of the ladies in the room. They all want a little ruffneck of their own.

"Must be the shoes," says Poo.

"No, I think it's the jiggy jeans," he says, tugging on his baggy denims.

Something clever comes to me at this point but my tongue gets tied. The ecstasy is making a second run on my senses and deploying units to my extremities. I notice a tingle in my groin. "You guys know where the bathroom's at in this place?," I ask.

"Down the hall to your right," answers Travis.

As I begin to make my way down the hall, I start rolling really hard, my legs turning to licorice and my eyes fluttering like a two bit whore. I arrive in the bathroom moments later, like I've been propelled through space and time, a good five minutes of my life taking off in a rented Caddy up ahead of me, waving goodbye and cheering me on.

"Ew-ah," hovering over the toilet.

It's really difficult to take a piss when I'm blowing up. All those muscles in my body, the involuntary ones, I forget what they're called, anyway, I take them for granted. With ecstasy, the rules change, it fucks with your wiring. I've noticed that all my voluntary muscles become reflexive, twitching, acting up, and the involuntary ones don't work for shit, and so I have to flex every muscle in my torso just to get a drop.

I turn the water on, hoping that will help, and tilt my head back, closing my eyes. Nothing. My whole body is numb, can't even feel my dick in my hand. I check really quick to make sure it's still there. It is. Then my eyes are drawn to a can of air freshener on the sink.

Contents..misused..can't read when I'm rolling either, so I pick it up to get a closer look..dangerous..inhaled.. Now there has to be a reason why they print that shit. It must pack a mean buzz. I shouldn't..ah, what the fuck...

Suddenly outside of my body, I see myself standing over the toilet, spraying air freshener up my nose. No doubt, it ranks up there as one of the most foolish, dope sick things I've ever done, the spray ripping into my sinuses, a fine mist blowing out the cracks of my eyesockets onto my face and into my hair..Potpourri.....and then darkness.

10

Somehow I wind up in a back room on an old, sunken-in sofa that smells of bongwater and cigarette ashes, rusted springs needling my back, and so I sit up.

The television is turned to a local music video show, public access or something because I recognize the dive that the current video was filmed in. It's Penis Envy doing "Leather (Whatever the Weather)". They're queer punk and very rad I might add. I caught them late last year with another queer punk band, Ballsack Opera, I think. I remember Penis Envy for their bassist who got arrested that night for doing a solo with his hard cock and jerking off on his guitar. Pretty impressive stuff.

I'm convinced that punk will never die, but continue to reinvent itself until the end of time. Working class rebellion. The art of making noise. The do-it-yourself ethic. Tomorrow's punk might not sound like today's, or yesterday's for that matter, but it's the attitude that matters.

Top five concerts of all time, my time that is, in no particular order, the Rolling Stones, Ministry at the second

Lollapalooza, Nine Inch Nails at the Woodstock anniversary, Pantera, and every punk rock show I've ever been to. Actually, I'll have to cheat a little - all the bands representing New York hardcore deserve a shout out too. We could all learn something from straight edge kids.

My Lollapalooza experience begs to be elaborated on..allow me to set the stage, no pun intended.

It is common knowledge that in the early 90's, right after Nirvana broke, America was fully on grunge's dick. Soundgarden could be heard thundering from the back of frat boys' jeeps all across the land and anyone who didn't own Pearl Jam's *Ten* wasn't worth the afterbirth they rode in on. Needless to say when the line-up for the second Lollapalooza was announced, the masses rejoiced. The two titans occupied the same bill, along with another crowd pleaser, The Red Hot Chili Peppers, who were also getting ready to explode with *Blood Sugar Sex Magic*. Throw in Ice Cube and you've got one hell of a party.

Ministry? Are they from Seattle? At the time, "Jesus Built my Hotrod" was about the only exposure most of the country had to Ministry. The track was gaining popularity at dance clubs, but Ministry was far more visible in goth/hardcore/industrial circles than in the mainstream, and I remember the day well.

I won't disclose how many tabs of acid I ate that afternoon, I fear Timothy Leary might roll over in his grave, but I digress...storm on the horizon, a large bank of opaque clouds hanging ominously over the stage and by the time the sun started to go down most of the flanneled freaks were worn out, hanging about breathlessly on their alt. rock playground, eagerly awaiting the Chili Peppers. Few had any idea what Ministry was about.

A few power chords later, a virtual army of crusty punks snapped quickly to attention. I'm sure it was the acid but I'd swear up and down many of them were literally born of the congealing mud on the ground, and after the first few licks of *Thieves* the place came unglued, a legion of rabid fans storming the stage. Some stopped short, just for a moment though, as if saying a silent prayer for their anti-heroes before stomping off to the pit; the rest didn't even hesitate.

I live for those types of situations, when it feels like the walls of social order could come down at any moment, controlled chaos, the potential for anarchy.

Woodstock was a similar experience. I went with some friends from work, representing the crew since none of them could arrange to disappear for an entire weekend.

I fed my mom some bullshit story, told her I was going water skiing, I think. I still get the chills when I think about the acid I ate that weekend. Damn near left my mind and my guts on that frickin' field. Shit tore me up. Had the time of my life though. In retrospect, that Saturday was probably the most memorable day of my young life....remembering B-Real from Cypress Hill, 'They call us Generation X. I say we're Generation Fuck You,' *right on,* 250,000 people chanting 'fuck the police'. My balls get tight just thinking about it.

The crowd at Woodstock had no intention of violence..matter of fact, I didn't see any all weekend, but it's not about violence, as much as it is strength in numbers.

How do you stop a quarter of a million people from starting a revolution?

"You know what I'm talkin' about, right bro?," comes a voice from the corner of the room.

It's dark, but by the fuzzy glow of the TV, I can make out several other people in the room..guy lookin' like a redneck with a razor blade, small mirror with some coke on it resting on his chest, a trashy girl with a crumpled up tissue with some blood on it in her hand, a bong at their feet, and on the couch with me, a kid who reminds me vaguely of a pre-adolescent

Mr. Potato Head, proudly displaying his dinner on his shirt. Draft beer. You can't win for losing.

I grab the remote off the table in front of me. *Friends.* Yuck. Must see T.V.? *Must flee T.V.*, I scoff as I change the channel belligerently and MTV's Singled Out flashes onto the screen...I can single handedly link MTV to the rising national debt. It was that blue light special on pop culture some years back. America is still paying for MTV. Sometimes I'm tempted to forgive them. After all, they did give us *Ren and Stimpy* and *Liquid Television*, making them responsible for *The Simpsons* in a roundabout sort of way, but then they do something really ridiculous like a throw a beach party with the cast of Baywatch. I'm sorry, but David Hasselhoff has, and always will be, Michael fucking Knight to me. I don't care how many Top 40 hits he has in Bangladesh.

Baywatch. A definitive sign of the impending pop culture apocalypse. In the end, all that will remain are the cockroaches and Pammie Anderson's implants. In a calculated attempt to save the bloodline, they will mate with every living organism on the face of the earth and the Silicon Age will be upon us. Barb Wire, queen of the New World Disorder.

No shit, they got HBO. Right on. Chris Rock is the man. Part of a whole new breed of comics that speak the truth. Comedy specials are about the only thing I mess with anymore on television. When I was younger, I wanted to be a comedian when I grew up. Comedians have all the power.

The girl's nose is beginning to bleed, trickling slowly down over her lips. I follow it down her chin and notice that her left breast is hanging out, and looking closer, I see that her panties are down around her knees, her skirt hiked up, exposing her privates. Bastard probably took advantage of her.

His eyes are glassy, conscious just long enough to do

another line, and then he notices the girl out of the corner of his eye, the blood running over her exposed chest. Startled, he grabs the tissue from her hand and dabs her nose and her breast, fondling it, as a twisted connection begins to form in my mind - the abuser and the care taker, what a sick world. Having never acknowledged that anyone was in the room to listen, he begins to speak again.

"You know how it works. You do some coke, smoke some bud, do some more coke, drink a beer, do some coke, smoke some coke, do some mor..uh.."

"What's up chief?," I ask sardonically.

"Wow. What a fucked up dream. Jesus was there. I—I—shit," he rubs his temples vigorously. This guy's definitely a F.O.G. operative. It was bound to happen sooner or later, someone would have to bring Jesus into it.

"I did bong swats with Jesus...and the Easter Bunny. Santa Claus was there too...fuckin' fiends dude. Jesus is the biggest pothead. His eyes were all puffy and red, and I skipped him once and he freaked, 'Skippin the son of God..I'm the man..skippin the man, skippin the man.' And the frickin rabbit and Santa kept repeating him, 'Skippin the man, skippin the man.' Then they left."

Silence. The man seems to have forgotten where he is, staring at the walls with a puzzled look on his face, like plaster was a new concept or something. Stupid people should *not* do drugs, "...fuuuuccckk, I need a bong swat."

He proceeds to take a frighteningly methodical hit from the bong, attempting to hold in the hit, smoke rolling slowly off his lips.

It seems rather ironic that the television is now tuned to Pat Robertson, carrying on from his pulpit about the same man, Jesus...his take on the whole thing is slightly different of course, as is mine. Religion seems to be the one thing that everyone has an opinion on.

To me, organized religion is not too much unlike any

other subculture phenomenon. Roman Catholics, Protestants, Atheists, Jews, all stand along side Deadheads, punk rockers, Satanists and others looking for something to believe in, searching for a greater purpose, for an identity. Religious organizations recruit with the promise of eternal salvation, other groups carve niches with music, drugs, fashion, a sense of belonging, it's all the same.

I was raised Catholic and confirmed a skeptic. I have strong beliefs, but I am hardly an active member of the church. Aside from all the recent sex scandal cases within the church, I have other reasons for maintaining my distance, the hypocrisy running much deeper. I've never felt comfortable with someone trying to tell me how to live my life. It seems like somewhere along the way the church forgot that Christ is an ideal, a model for action, not a mandate. To expect human beings to be Christ-like or risk eternal damnation is the mother of all guilt trips. There's no A for effort in the Catholic church. I'm the best person I can be everyday and that's not good enough? I thought as Christians we were supposed to be nonjudgmental and yet the church judges me; a crucial dogmatic flaw that has never been addressed and probably never will be.

The sermon from the mount continues...

"It makes sense if you think about it, I mean, Jesus bein' a stoner and all. He was always hittin' the bottle. Jesus loved wine man, who's to say he didn't enjoy an occasional smoke?," he ponders, laughing, coughing and expelling the rest of the smoke from his lungs.

"He ate a shit load of bread. Munchies, man..that's prolly why the last dinner was so damn big," hack, hack. "That kid was always promoting peace and love, love thy neighbor...shit, that set the entire foundation for joint etiquette," hack.

"Yeah, no shit," I mumble, hoping to satiate him. No luck.

"He told me a story dude."

"Who told you a story?"

"Jesus did. He wants everybody to know why he turned over all those tables in the market. 'Member that, like the bible says?"

"Uh..yeah."

"There was no head shop dude. Jesus freaked..then he started talkin' some crazy shit about flea markets in Jersey. The twelve disciples...hitmen, dude. *Hired guns*. They had like a cartel and shit, ran the drug trade in the holy town. Jerusalem was corrupt as hell."

I begin nodding slowly, putting him in a trance, his eyes trying to focus on me, crossing towards the bridge of his nose, as I rock back and forth.

After a few moments, he passes back out and I flip through the channels, surfing to the local news, to three dead in a murder-suicide on the other side of town. It would suck to be dead. My mind wanders, and I think about all of the things I'd miss on the other side..my family, my friends, and all the little things too, sunsets, cheeseburgers, a cold beer...a girl I know pondered whether she would have access to drugs after she died and she figured 'yes' because heaven is all about your favorite things and hell is all about being bad, so you win either way.

Speaking of winning, or losing rather, the Magic basketball game is on. Never been too into sports myself. I can't identify with that competitive mentality..team sports gave me a complex as a kid, the pressure to perform, to be the best, but like everything in life, it all comes back down to believing in something...since there's a young boy in Kansas who's self esteem resides solely in his ability to dunk a basketball, and right down the street there's another, slightly older and past his prime, who has only one thing in life to look forward to, the NFL on Sunday afternoons. I suppose that all of America's most banal pastimes serve some higher purpose like that.

"Ral-ly, ral-ly," I joke to myself, somehow finding the strength to lift myself from the couch.

I'm really dragging. The coke on the mirror. It would probably get me home at least. I don't do coke though, I've never done coke. I'll just do a little and take even less with me, for later.

Picking up the empty vial at their feet, I scoop up a pinch of the dust and deposit it, then take two pinches for myself, sniffing them off my fingertips. Nothing. I thought coke hit right away. More. I pick up the straw and cut out a line with the razor, snorting it up quickly, but silently, trying hard not to disturb Bonnie and Clyde. They stir, but fall short of waking.

After putting everything back in place, I stand still for a moment, staring at the television, waiting for something to happen. Cocaine. Colombia's entire economy revolves around on this shit? Scarface killed for this shit? John Belushi died for this shit? Do they know something I don't know?

The Other Side

astral ecstasy amongst the people of the nebula
nocturnal where the rain rocks the spectrum of
cosmic bliss setting the sky on fire with the colors
of life eternal where the river meets the sky in
the land of blue sunsets the land of yellow seas
where the children of the universe frolic on the
electric playground at the edge of time and all
that was all that is and all that will be share a
cup of tea while the sun sets in a far away place
on the Other Side.

11

Next thing I know, I'm in the back seat of my Jetta, sandwiched between Poo and Chad, evil trance oozing from the tape player, a Moontribe DJ, Daniel maybe, reality having fallen away again, awash in waves of unconsciousness with no real sense of time or place...definitely my car, but the edges of the picture are fuzzy and distorted, tunnel vision times ten thousand, but ecstasy is weird like that; on acid everything seems so angular and shapely, so crisp. I reach out and lightly rub the seats, making sure they're really there.

Chad stirs next to me and I turn to look at him. His face is slack, he's grinding his teeth. Grabbing my knee and rubbing my leg, he attempts to speak but the thoughts die each time he opens his mouth..like 'Can-'..and 'Shhh-'..and 'Mmm-'.."Fu-ck dude. What's goin' on?," I ask. "Blowing the fuck up dude," he manages.

Looking around the car, the bottom drops out of my stomach. They're all blowing up. Hard. Even Trav, in the driver's seat. "Damn dude. What the fuck are you guys thinkin' eatin' the rest of those pills?," I sound like a surfer on Quaaludes, thoughts barely rolling off the tip of my tongue. "Was your idea bro," says Chad through clenched teeth. "Huh?"

"Said you were lovin' it. Asked for more."

"More? I ate muh..?"

Every time I begin to form a complete sentence in my head, the trancey beats spilling from the speakers in the back change directions menacingly, like a shark's fin in psychedelic waters, and I lose my train of thought.."Trav, can you turn that down bro?"

"..two like the rest of us."

"What?"

"Yeah," repeats Chad casually. Bursts of frenzied conversation are followed by extended chemical silences. "Man, I don't remember anything. I did some coke to-"

"Coke? That shit you had in your pocket?," he asks. "Yeah," I say. "That's K bro, not coke. How much did you do?," he asks. "A line," I say innocently, and "a fucking line?!", but "shit dude, the guy kept talkin' about coke and I-"

"He was probably tryin' to come down. Christ Dan, you're lucky you're not dead."

It's hard to say how much time has passed, minutes, hours, could be days for all I know. I poke my head between the two front seats to get a better look at Travis. His eyes are half-shut, his pupils hidden beneath the lids, and I look at the speedometer. We're only going ten miles an hour. "Shit Trav, you all right to drive?," I ask, not really caring what the answer is since I sure as hell wasn't going to. "You're only goin' ten miles an hour."

"I know. Feels like 80 though, don't it," he observes, turning his head slowly to look at me. "Where are we?"

"Following this chick to a party in the ghetto."

"Whose party?"

"Hell if I know bro, think she might live there with some dude that Jason knows." Jason stirs in the passenger seat after hearing his name.

"Oh shit. Hey Dan, what up kid?," he asks, startled, sedated.

"Nada bro. Fucked up."

"Yeah, no shit dude, I'm torqued, Unspecial K in those pills too I think... whatever happened to good old fashioned MDMA?"

I plop my ass back into my seat and close my eyes, reeling from the E. When the E is good, it's amazing, but when it's bad, it really sucks.

"This isn't the same shit you gave me early."

"No, we bought some more," says Chad.

"From who?," I ask. "From Charles," he says.

"No shit, wud you do that for? God only knows what's in these pills."

"You want some coke for real, to straighten you out?"

Straighten me out? The rationale behind mixing drugs is so backwards. Up, down, up, down - a sinister statement on the mindset of a junkie..justifying the depth of the valleys, with the height of the peaks. "Yeah," I decide.

Chad pulls a vial out of his pocket and holds it up, checking to see how much is left. Then he loads a bump for me and holds it to my nose. "Sniff Dan, sniff."

"I know bro. I know."

"Well, we're almost there," he says anxiously.

The ghetto, sort of a pet name we have for the area just between the majority of the student housing in the city and the true ghetto..lower income housing, but not quite the projects.

We park on the street in front of the party..kickin', cars as far as I can see, people hanging out in the street and the yard, mad flow like a tractor beam from the back..*my name is Bootie Brown and I'm proceeding, leading, they try to follow but they shallow and hallow, I can see right through them, like an empty 40 bottle of O.E., the Pharcyde...right on, I like* this party already.

Suddenly I like it even better as a gorgeous blond emerges from the car in front of us and joins us in smoking a joint at the driver's side window. Long, fine strawberry blond hair with puppy dog brown eyes and a pretty smile, she takes a pull from the joint and sticks her head through the window, blowing the smoke sensually into Travis's open mouth. "Hey Dan." She winks at me as Travis expels the second-hand smoke from his lungs.

She's the kind of chick that doesn't even bother to front like she's not a slut, she knows she is; it's written all over her face that she likes to fuck. I wonder how she knows my name. Must have met her earlier after I blacked out.
"I'm sorry. What was your name again?," I ask, with as much civility as possible, rubbing my nose.
"Kelly."

She sticks her head in the window again and starts making out with Travis, one eye on me in the back seat. I'm jealous. Of Travis. And her. Damn, it's been a long time since I got laid. "Let's do this boys," suggests Jason, opening the passenger side door.

Smoke rolls out onto the grass as we exit. Poo is passed out so we leave him in the back seat and head for the party. It's the usual heterogeneous bunch of students, skaters, ravers, addicts, freaks; hard to tell what everybody's on, but I notice a lot of plastic cups, some in hands, even more on the ground, so there must be a keg somewhere.

The air is thick with smoke inside, the crowd subdued and sparse, a small group of people on the couch nodding their heads to Roni Size, passing a bong back and forth which reaches me in no time but dies in my hands. I pack a fresh bowl from my stash, fire it up and then pass it on. After Travis and Kelly hit it once, she leads him away by the hand towards the back of the house...guy on the couch to my right is the most animated of the lot, choking on an oversized hit. "You all right dude?," I ask. "Yeah," choke, "fine", hack, "chillin", choke.

Bad move on my part because once you get a speed freak talkin' to ya, there's no shutting him up. This guy proceeds to share with me everything I always *didn't* want to know about his love affair with dope - about how he would find ways to smoke buds even if he lost all his limbs, and so limb by limb, he breaks it down for me rambling on about a roach clip that's designed to fit on his big toe, a bong harness for his shoulders, contraption for his ass crack..he loses me quickly, talking a mile a minute. "Yeah dude, and the grow room's kickin'."

"Oh yeah, what's your secret?"

He launches into a dissertation on the biology of hydroponics. Lights, ventilation, males, females, clones, zygots, zygotes..he loses me again, his antics intensified by his outrageous appearance, skinny, like a toothpick, big, bloodhsot eyes and a huge head like his neck could snap any second from the weight, though his ears would cushion the fall. They're enormous.

I recognize the guy across from me from Chemistry class. His name is Ricky, but everyone calls him Filter because he constantly lights the wrong end of his cigarette when he gets fucked up.

"What's up Ricky?"

"Hey..oh, hey Danny.."

Ricky's not exactly the brightest bulb in the place. He's holding a can of Budweiser in his hand and smoking a Marlboro.

"Hey bro..you're ashing in your beer."

"Huh?," as he takes a sip.

"You just ashed your cigarette in your beer."

He laughs and nods his head.

Moron.

"You know what the real secret is though?," continues speed

boy.

"Oh, you were gettin' to that?"

"Yeah, yeah, I sing to 'em," he says. "To what?"

"To my plants man. Mostly showtunes, but it's fucked up, lately they've been responding to hair bands," he laughs speedily. "Huh?"

"Yeah, isn't that crazy? You know that one part of that Motley Crue song? That da-da-dananana," he hums, playing air guitar. "Umm.."

"Too Young to Fall in Love, yeah, that's the one, da-da-dananana," he says, getting excited. "Yeah, they grow mad crazy when I play that song for 'em."

"No shit."

"And you know what else works well? Fart spray dude...spray that shit right on them bad boys and you'll have buds for days."

Finally, I decide I've had enough of the Beavis routine and excuse myself to go to the bathroom, heading outside instead. There's two kegs flowing in the backyard. I grab a cup laying on the ground nearby and get in line, overhearing a conversation about the X going around, and speculation that heroin is the secret ingredient in the latest batch, low grade heroin at that. The guy in front of me slowly turns around.

"Danny," he exclaims with excitement. "What the fuck's goin' on?"

"Hey Gavin," I answer, recognizing his face as one of Chad's old wrestling buddies.

"How you been?," I ask.

"Good bro. Good. Gonna be a big senior next year so I'm stoked. How's Biz?"

Biz, short for "biziness", is Chad's unofficial nickname compliments of his devoted customers. "Chad's fine dude. He's inside actually."

"Oh yeah. No shit."

"Yeah. Jason and Travis too," I say competently, the coke having mended my slack tongue.

"Wow, you got all your boys out tonight huh?"

"Well this is it. We all go our separate ways on Friday," I say edgily, unsure of where to take the conversation from here.

"Hey, you talk to Eddie lately? He got his shit back together or what?"

"No, you didn't hear dude?"

"Hear what?," I ask, suddenly concerned about my old friend.

"Eddie passed away a couple weeks ago. Heroin overdose." Not so thirsty for a beer anymore.

"The big H," he repeats, smacking his forearm. Dizzy.

"Smackola." Short of breath.

"The white horse," his words echoing surreally through my head. Feel like I'm going to be sick.

"You all right Dan?"

"Yeah, fine," I say, choking on my tongue. "I have to go to the bathroom."

I rush inside and down the hall to the bathroom. Locking the door, I fall to my knees and stick my head in the toilet as violent spasms rack my body, dry heaves, nothing in my stomach to throw up except spittle, mucous and something darker, blood maybe. I cling to the toilet for several minutes, allowing the spasms to subside. I can see myself in the full length mirror on the back of the door. Pathetic. I look like shit, like I'm made of the crap that I just spit up.

The war in my head rages on. I, the revolutionary, have infiltrated their camp. I spy, click..click..the tiny camera in my mind's eye documents the battle plan of their self destructive dictator, his heinous plot being to exploit my fears and doubts, my vices and insecurities, rub salt on my wounds, my weaknesses. The thought police are not far behind, sent to manipulate me and rob me of my will. Temptation and trickery around every corner.

I sit on the floor for several minutes, staring at my reflection, trying to convince myself that I'm not a bad person, that it's circumstance, that I'm in control, that I won't end up like Eddie.

"Hey, you fall in pal?," somebody pounds on the door.

"Uh..I'll be out in a sec."

I stand up and turn on the water at the sink, splashing water on my face and in my mouth. There's some Scope in the medicine cabinet. I take a cap full to get the taste of bile out of my mouth, then I towel off my face and open the door, passing several people waiting in a line to use the bathroom. Time to go out and get some fresh air. Back in the living room, I round up Jason and Chad.

"You guys wanna go for a walk?," I ask them, flashing a joint to get their attention.

I pause right outside the front door and take a deep breath of the night air, Chad and Jason following closely behind me. Crossing to the other side of the road, opposite the street lights, we walk slowly from the party. I light the joint, taking a hit and passing it to Jason. "Danny, you all right? You look like you just saw a ghost," says Chad with concern.

"I'm cool, just got a little sick is all."

"Oh, really? That's hated."

"I'll live."

We continue smoking the joint in silence, pausing momentarily while Jason ties his shoe, and it occurs to me that we haven't been paying any attention to where we're walking. We've only covered about four blocks, but our surroundings have grown increasingly grim. I guess we were a little closer to the ghetto then we thought.

"You guys know how to get back?," I ask.

"We'll just follow the music," suggests Jason.

At that exact moment, the music in the distance stops abruptly, with the squeal of a record being scratched. Bad karma. It starts back up for a second and then stops again.

Starts up, stops. Starts up, stops, this time with the thump and sizzle of a woofer being blown to shreds. "Got any other ideas?"

12

There's a light on in a driveway up ahead. I wouldn't think too much of it, except it's the only light I've seen for the last two blocks. The sound of sneakers shuffling around on concrete carries on the wind as we approach a group of tough looking white boys playing shirts and skins basketball in the driveway of a rundown, two story house. The game stops as we stroll by.

"Whatchu smokin', bro?"

"Herb."

"You got any for sale?," asks the larger one of the group, walking towards us.

"Kiss my ass," answers Jason snidely, hitting the joint casually. "What?!"

"I said kiss my ass, homes. Back to your bricks."

The kid nods his head, a scowl forming on his face.

"I got one for your head, motherfucker."

"Bring it on," calls Jason over his shoulder.

They stare us the rest of the way down the street and then return to their game as we dip down the first side street we come to. "What the hell was that, dude?"

"Fuck them."

"A simple 'no' woulda done the trick, ya think?"

"Whatever bro, if they were for real they woulda done something about it back there."

"They got nothin' to lose.."

Jason walks off ahead of me and says something but I can't hear him. My knees go weak with a long forgotten memory of a hot day, steam rising from the concrete, and the bell ringing loudly behind me as I awkwardly hustled my pre-pubescent body out to the bike cage at Thomas Downey Middle School. We had just moved from Ohio to Florida weeks before, and for the first time in my life I was attending a public school.

My second week, I saw a girl get hooked like a fish to a water faucet, wet steel ripping through her cheek. Her attacker got suspended and I wondered what punishment murder would bring - *detention?* There was always bloody, violent fights after school and since I had no friends to stick around and socialize with, I was usually in a hurry to get home.

In Ohio, I never owned a chain, but after two bikes disappeared in a month, my mom decided it was time to starting locking up. It was a heavy chain, with a padlock on the end, and as I was removing it, there was a commotion. Two kids shouted each other, using language I had never heard before, and then a fight broke out.

"Yo, give me that chain, dog," and a third guy was practically on top of me.

I didn't know what else to do but give it to him. I thought about throwing it, but my whole body was shaking miserably and I honestly feared for my life.

He joined the melee, attacking a light haired kid from behind. I remember he had light hair because of the contrast when the dark red, almost black blood ran down the back of his head. I wanted to cry, or run, but instead I just watched.

103

I spent the next day in the principal's office being interrogated about the incident. They wanted to know why I gave up my chain, and they badgered me about it until I cried. The whole experience upset me a great deal, to the point where I had to miss school over it. Then my dad turned it around. "Son...you did the right thing. Don't ever mess with someone with nothing to lose." And not only did it make a lot of sense, but it made me feel important, like I had a lot to lose.

"Kid's been watching too many Rap City Videos," notices Chad.

The side street takes us deeper into the ghetto so we turn at the next street and head north, back in the direction of the party. "Why don't you grab Trav so we can leave?," Chad suggests.

We stop at Trav's car to check on Poo, still sleeping soundly in the back seat. I rap my knuckles on the window, but he doesn't stir. "You guys think he's all right?"

"He's fine bro. He had a lot to drink," says Chad.

Before heading back inside, I slyly snort the rest of the K I have..hadn't noticed how fast my heart was racing from the coke until I smoked that joint, like it could leap right out of my chest. Hopefully the K will slow it down. Feel like I'm playing dodgeball with panic again.

The party has thinned out considerably. I step into the back hallway and shamelessly eavesdrop on Travis and Kelly. There's laughter coming from her bedroom, and something smells good - opium. The door is cracked so I stick my head through, hoping for an invite. "Dan, come on in," says Kelly, in a very animated tone.

Trav and Kelly sit on the bed blowing bubbles through wands. I take a seat on the floor and Travis passes me a small pipe. I hit it once. Then again. Tasty.

"Travis and I were just talkin' about how strange it would be if the world was full of bubbles," Kelly explains, giggling.

"Wouldn't it be though? Strange..if God had a huge wand in

the sky and blew big bubbles all day, everywhere you go, bubbles in the air. Big ones. Small ones," she says, amused.

I smile, distracted, only half listening as Trav plays along with her, a sly look in his eyes, like he's just waiting for the right moment to pounce on her. I'd pay good money for a ring side seat to that. They'd be hot together. Kelly is fine, and I'd love to see Travis in action. I take another hit from the pipe.

"Dan, you all right? You don't look so hot."

"You remember Eddie bro? Used to wrestle for Boone. Dated Donna."

"Yeah, I saw him last month actually. You were there..."

"Where?"

"..that party with Rabbit in the Moon and Dimitri."

"Dead bro," I say flatly. "Died of a heroin overdose last week."

"No way," Travis states in shock. "Ed was straight as an arrow I thought."

Eddie had a rather extreme personality. He was very much alive, maybe *too* alive, driven to take all the things he cared about to the next level. Wrestling. His friendships. His relationship. I imagine that passion extended to his excesses. "Ahh..I don't know dude," I confess, stammering a bit, the opium spanking my brain. "Heard he'd fallen in with some freaks. Doesn't take long to graduate to heroin anymore."

"That's fucked up. What's up wit' the H lately? That shit ain't worth it."

The opium's making me feel faint. Mellow acid jazz leaks from two speakers on a bureau. A saxophone blows and spidery horns extend hairy legs, pulling me into their web.

Pushing myself up against the wall, I attempt to hold myself up, but it's no use...I catch brief glimpses of Trav and Kelly's faces, asking me if I'm all right, but spiraling once again towards the other side, I can't answer. Up, down, right, left, all abstract concepts to me, much like speaking or moving. To the unfortunate many of who've been there, it's affectionately known as a K hole.

I'm stalked by the chemical banshees in my head, mortified at the control which they seek to gain, ashamed at that which is no longer mine.

The rest of the night unfolds like a dream. In and out of varying states of consciousness, I'm treated to a show of sorts. Travis and Kelly are both naked, their bodies moving rhythmically under the sheets. She moans softly in pleasure as Trav's exposed ass lifts and falls slowly..God, Travis has a nice ass, and she has her hands all over it too. Bitch. Should be me. I cough loudly at one point, startling them. Travis looks at me and smiles mischievously, almost as if daring me to come to bed and join the two of them. "Wanna come play Danny?," Kelly asks me.

"Come here for a second Dan," instructs Travis.

I can't move a single muscle in my body. Fuck. I curse myself. Travis leans over the side of the bed and grabs me by the back of the head, kissing me deeply. I can't even move my tongue to meet his. Shit. I'm going to be kicking myself for months over this one. "You all right bro?," he asks me, looking into my eyes.

If I could only make it to the bed, but I'm dead weight, not a chance. Travis kisses me again and I suck on his lip for a moment before he returns his attention to Kelly..I'd love to fuck her while Travis watches, wanting me to do the same to him. Now she's on top, riding Travis hard, bucking to the bass pulsating through the door. Like page after page from *The Joy of Sex*, Travis fucks Kelly all night long while I lay watching, hard as a rock, missing out on the most amazing sexual experience of my life.

I stop at the last rung on the climb out of the K hole, loud voices coming from the other room, like there's some kind of commotion. I somehow manage to stand up and stagger out of the room....walls in the hallway appear to be breathing, tunnel vision, trouble focusing, wavy, like I'm in a funhouse and the floor is slanted..the voices becoming clearer. One of them is Jason's, but I can't make out what he's saying, just know that he's drunk, and then I hear a voice I don't recognize.

"What do I got? What do I got? Trauma for your drama, punk ass."

When I reach the end of the hall and enter the living room, I see Jason swaying in front of a small, but intimidating kid in an LA Raiders Starter jacket, a black cap turned to the side and baggies. He's poking Jason in the forehead, our friend from earlier at his side. "Why you tryin' me? Bitch ass piece a shit," he says angrily, spittle leaping from his mouth. "Fuck you," Jason snaps, jostling the kid.

He's got a gun in his hand, like it appeared out of nowhere, and now it's in Jason's mouth, the metal clattering against his teeth. The kid's pulling him close, jabbing the gun down his throat. Shit..I start to move forward. Suddenly feeling dizzy again, I put my hand on the wall to steady myself, but before I can act one way or another, the fucker's braining him, the butt of the gun landing solidly several times on Jason's forehead, his face catching the edge of a table on the way down.....a lot of blood and lot of movement. I see Chad rush to Jason's side, and then for the third time in as many hours, I black out.

respect! the endangered species
someone blinked now extinct
obscurity of sense past tense
2 far gone
pipe dream to pipe bomb
nine lives to nine millimeter
preacher to sinner air thinner
five feet forward six feet under
stolen thunder time to wonder
why?

Under the Gun

13
10:00 am, Monday morning

My senses are a wake up call, awake long before me, but I can't open my eyes..something smells like..roses? A casket?...pitter patter of rain over my head triggers a macabre slide show in my mind's eye—desolate graveyard and a lone casket, next, close up of the only mourner present, myself, close up of a tombstone with my name on it, misspelled, next, the heavens open up and the rain begins to fall, next, close up of the casket...

At this point, the slide burns through and the casket begins to fill with rain water, flooding through the cracks and turning the earth underneath to mud, swallowing up the casket.

I wake with a start, banging my head on the steering wheel of my car. Ripping down my Simpsons air freshener from my rear view, I place it against my nose; roses, and I toss it out the window. Travis must have dumped me here on his way home last night. The sun is up, but it's raining.

Jason..I have to find out if Jason's all right. My legs

give out as I attempt to get out of the car. I fall to the ground and lay there for a moment, letting the rain wash over my face, refreshing, but I'm getting soaked, so I pull myself up from the ground using the open car door for support, then slam it loudly, collapsing against it.

One of our neighbors drives by slowly, staring at me with a look somewhere between concern and pity. Like a deer caught in the headlights, I wave shyly and make an effort to stand up straight as she continues down the street, following me with her eyes in the rear view mirror. Time to take the show inside.

I make it halfway across the front lawn when my legs get tangled up underneath me and I fall again...what the hell is wrong with me? I've never felt so ate up in my life..definitely some funk in those pills.

Crawling the rest of the way across my yard, I open the door, my body spilling into the front hallway - silence - chilled air greets my wet skin, nauseated, but not head nausea, a sickening all over nausea, like somebody shot me up with cotton candy and cream corn through a dirty syringe..clutching my abdomen, the phone rings and the machine answers.

"Hey kiddo. Sorry I had to leave you in your ride, but you couldn't come up with a key and I didn't want your mom to see you like that, uh, oops..well let's hope she's not home to hear this. Hi Ms. Boyle. I've been at the hospital most of the morning, don't know how much you remember but Jason got in a fight and busted his head open. Had to get 10 stitches on his grill. He looks like the bride of Frankenstein, but he'll live. I'm exhausted bro, need to sleep for a bit, but I'll try you back later. If it keeps raining, we'll go shroomin' tonight, if you're up for it." Click.

The sound of the receiver crashing down on Trav's end sends me into a deep sleep right there on the hard wood floor and I'm transported back to the party last night. Jason.

A gun. Shouting. Next thing I know, Jason's brains are on the wall. Caps left and right. Chad goes down. Poo goes down.

Then the scene rewinds in my head.

In the background, a hardcore track from the night before burns on in my head, then ignites like a roman candle over the void, setting the stage for the madness to follow. This time, Jason gets the steel on the bridge of his nose but there's no blood as his head crashes into the table; instead it splits open, exposing his brain, which splits again and sends hundreds of pills flying across the room as everybody scatters, his body disintegrating into a towering pile of pills..some chick dives in, tossing them into the air and inviting others to join her...several guys jumping around the room like ballerinas, graceful with their toes extended, catching the pills with their mouths in mid air, swallowing them down and then exploding in flight, more pills raining down upon the room.

I fall to the ground, desperately picking up as many as I can in the hopes of putting Jason back together, but I pick one up and drop two, pick two up, drop four, pick four up, drop eight. This continues at a maddening pace for what seems like an eternity, until I am finally able to awaken myself, breaking the trance and sitting straight up on the floor in a cold sweat.

Pushing the door shut behind me, I stand up and launch my body at the bathroom, grabbing the toilet seat with both hands. My stomach is balled up in a knot, churning and bucking, and my head swims with nausea again. I stick my finger down my throat, gagging, and then throw up several times.

I feel better, but *better* is such a relative term at this point. Cleaning my face off, I proceed to my bedroom and fall to the floor, breathing deeply and trying to focus. Music. *I need something mellow.* Even jazz would sound like speed metal at this point.

I pop open my player to see what's inside. Dee-Lite.

It will have to do. I turn the volume down low and crawl into bed.

I want your lovin'. I need your lovin'...

Her haunting voice leads me into a deep sleep and then falls behind, trailing me into the woods..*I'll be your friend, I'll be your lover*..wafting through the trees, and I run, deeper into the darkness. Then the voice becomes distorted, the bass line like a doppleganger, soothing to grating to almost non-existent, like a heart in cardiac arrest. My feet become stuck to the ground, able to move only an inch at a time, knowing that whatever is behind is gaining quickly.

I stumble on a large root and fall. As I hit the ground, the footfalls stop abruptly. All is quiet. I stand slowly, brushing myself off, and the beast attacks from a branch above, dragging me back to the ground. I struggle, digging my fingernails into it's hairy back, biting and scratching, but it is strong and threatens to overpower me.

Clawing at it's back, my fingers sink into its skin and I am able to grab hold of its spine. It does not occur to me to break its back with my hands. Instead, I slowly make my way up from the base to where its flesh hangs loosely over the back of its brain like a mask, and I pull the skin forward.

To my horror, I find myself staring back at me. My eyes are shifty like a ventriloquist's dummy, my mouth hinged to my face, dangling open, and as I scream, the dummy screams back at me.

Wake up Dead

Do what's right
Right or wrong?
Wrong turn
Turn and fight
Fight the power
Power trip
Trip and fall
Fall asleep
Sleep now wake
Wake up dead
Dead man walking
Walking wounded
Wounded dying
Dying slowly
Slowly fading
Fading fast
Faster
FASTER.

14

The subconscious freak show continues for what seems to be an eternity, then stops suddenly and I fall into a deep sleep.

It's dark out when I awake to a long line of spit wrapped around my head. Must have accidentally cranked the AC instead of killing it, feels like its ten below in my room so I get out of bed and check the thermostat in the living room. I had dropped it as far as it would go, to 55 degrees, charging down to about 63. Shuddering and rubbing my naked skin, I hurry back to my bedroom and get under the sheets. Warmth. The rain is still coming down outside. It puts me back to sleep in an instant. For an instant. The phone is ringing. "Hello.."

"Danny boy, it's Greg. We're coming over. Gotta get to the fields before every freak in the city raids our stash. Are you down?"

"Those pills left me gooey as fuck dude."

"I hear ya bro. I was sick all morning."

"Well, why don't we just chill today?"

"Cuz it's been raining for hours, we have to-"

"Do I have a choice?"

"Danny, as Americans we all have choices. We choose life or death, Democrat or Republican, fried or broiled, to be a wuss or n-", I hang up, lunatics, every last one of them.

I rip the sheets away from my body and expose myself to the air hoping to wake myself, then head for the bathroom to take a shower. I can hear my mom fumbling with her keys at the front door. By the time I am finished, she is all ready fixing dinner in the kitchen. "Danny," she calls from the kitchen as I step out into the hallway.

"Yeah mom."

"You going to have some dinner before you go out?"

"Uh," don't really have time for dinner but, "sure."

"It'll be ready in about five minutes."

"O.K.," I call back.

I was going to wear all black for the shrooming expedition, but decide to pack a bag instead. I stop short on the way to the kitchen and watch my mom from afar. She looks so angelic standing over the stove, stirring the sauce for our pasta. A lump forms in my throat.

She's been working so hard since my father died, so strong, and full of so much love. So beautiful; inside and out. I really wish she could find someone to share the rest of her life with.

It would be impossible to wear my heart on my sleeve these days, heavy as it is. It's not only the love that I have for her, or the love that she has for me, but the utter disregard for her feelings that come with my actions, jeopardizing my own well-being on a regular basis when I know how crushed she would be if anything ever happened to me. Sometimes I hate myself for it, and for being so conscious of the dynamics at work and feeling so powerless against them.

"All four food groups, did you notice?," she asks. "No, I didn't."

"If you count the tomatoes in the sauce," she says beaming.

"Gotcha."

"How are you?," she asks, with genuine interest.

"Not too bad. Been hangin' with the guys a lot, went to a rave-"

"I said how are you Dan. How *are* you? O.K.?"

"Fine," I say, nose in my plate.

"Are you sure? I mean, I care what you've been up to, where you've been too, but more important is that everything is O.K. It's not like you to disappear for days at a time."

"Well, I'm leaving at the end of the week. Just trying to spend as much time with the guys as I can."

The drugs have driven a wedge between us. I always feel ashamed when I'm around her, guilty, edgy, like she raised me better and I'm letting her down.

"Dan, you don't look well though. You've been sitting at the table for less than five minutes and you've eaten enough pasta to feed a small family. Are you eating?"

Once she puts me on the defensive, I shut down - fight or flight and I always spread my wings. I respect my mother too much to fight with her. I know I have a problem, she doesn't need to know, I'll handle it, I tell myself. It's starting to put distance between us though. We don't talk like we used to.

"Dan. Are you eating?" Saved by the bell. The crew minus Jason is at the door. I let them in and they follow me into the kitchen to get my bag and jacket.

"Are you going to spend any time with your mother this week before you leave me forever?," the edge has left her voice.

"I'm not leaving you forever mom."

"I know, I'm just giving you a hard time," she says, smiling lovingly. "So where you off to now?"

"We're going to the movies."

"Whatcha going to see?"

"Uh..that new Stallone flick."

"Which one is that?"

"I don't know. They're all the same anyway," I say.

"Yeah, right," says Travis, backing me up.

"O.K., well have fun. We have a lot to do before you leave on Friday Dan. Can you pencil me in for tomorrow?"

"You know Danny Ms. Boyle, Mr. Procastration," blurts Poo, catching Chad's hand on the back of his head.

"Oh really Dan? I didn't know you were an advocate," says my mom with incredible timing, fighting to suppress a laugh.

"What did I say?"

"It's procrastination bro."

"Yeah, like I said, procastration," says Poo, rubbing the back of his head.

Everyone in the room shares a laugh.

"I love you babe," says mom, hugging me and kissing me on the forehead.

"Love you too," I say, beating a hasty retreat. "Don't wait up for me, O.K. I might be late."

"What else is new? Bye boys," she says, waving as we leave.

On the way to the fields, we slam a twelve pack and smoke a joint. The ride usually takes about an hour, but we're there in about half of that time thanks to Chad, the speed freak. Parking right out in the open, with the hazard lights on in the middle of the road, he pulls out a box of paper bags to collect the booty with, and several flashlights.

We reach the other side of the fence and scramble in different directions, our lights playing across the ground...first couple of chips I stumble upon have all ready been flipped which means one of two things: either someone raided the field earlier or the cows are tripping their udders off. What a sensational headline that would make.. *Country's Milk Supply Tainted by Hedonistic Cows...*

I can see the media flocking to that one, setting up

camp around old man Townsend's ranch, chasing him down for a comment as he feeds his pigs at sunrise.

"Well, I always just fig'ed they was like dogs and stuff. Dogs won't have nuttin' do with they own dung. Them there cows tho take to they own shit like flies to, er uh, bees to honey. Darndest thing I ever did see."

"So you were aware your cows were using psychedelics?"

"No, I don't reckon I thought no how of it."

Correspondent Ronald Shaw is on location live with Bessie the cow.

"So you're saying this *wasn't* a secret plot in conjunction with the Rainbow family to usher in a new era of peace and love, and facilitate a new interest in and revival of 60's counter culture values?"

"Man, do I look like a hippie to you?"

"And the accusations flying that it was indeed deliberate?"

"Two words - cow tipping."

"Do you have anything else to say for yourself?"

"Got milk?," moos Bessie, shimmying with uncontrollable laughter...I laugh to myself as I continue combing the grass. The better piles are always closer to the house, but I try to avoid getting too close if at all possible. I've heard too many stories from friends about picking rock salt from Mr. Townsend's shotgun out of their bruised asses. One guy I know even caught some in the eye once and had to go to the hospital. Townsend can lick my ass though. What's he going to do with the shrooms? Not a damn thing. What a waste.

It's starting to look like approaching the house is my only option. All the chips that haven't been flipped are either too old to support life or have been picked clean. I think for a moment about calling out to the boys to see if they're having better luck, but decide that it's probably not a good idea.

Then I spot it - the motherlode, a towering pile of shit with dozens of delicious, purple ringed beauties sprouting from it. Pulling the bag from my back pocket, I begin picking them from the dung, eating one for every three that I put in the bag..kinda over-the-top I suppose, eating shrooms right from the crap, but in my drunken stupor, I don't even think twice. For several moments, I scour the ground feverishly. There's several smaller piles even closer to the house, all of which contain life. I can hear the guys goofing off at the other end of the field, probably flinging turds at each other. Some wise ass, usually Jason, always starts trouble. I've never been able to figure out the whole connection between adolescent boys and shit. As a kid, I remember the joy I would find in blowing up dog shit with firecrackers and launching it at girls with a slingshot. Boys will be boys I guess.

It has grown progressively darker since we came over the fence and in my eagerness to get to the best the field has to offer, I hardly realize how much time has passed. I can feel the buzz rolling in, like storm clouds approaching, the blue turns slowly to gray, and the world begins to melt...I take a seat in attempt to steady myself, and as I stretch out on the ground, psychedelia comes calling.

Looking towards the sky and out across the field, I enter the realm of dots, the physical world around me falling away into a swirling malestorm of atoms and molecules.

It's that intangible something in the night air. The sky is electric. Not black, not purple, but a warm blue. Shadows fall on the ground nearby. As the wind begins to blow, the shadows dance like marionettes, their strings manipulated by some otherworldly force. With the soft earth as their stage, they assume their roles. Some as trees and rocks, while the others take on less familiar, more alien roles. Then the wind dies down abruptly, almost arrogantly. It's as if the wind holds the secrets of the night, unwilling to divulge them. Slowly it gives in, whispering to the trees as it wafts through their branches, giving up *the secrets. Suddenly, the night is alive. All of nature seems to revel in its newfound knowledge and sense of purpose. The wind begins to howl, letting all know that it has the power. Without the wind, the secrets of the night could not be conveyed. It is the courier of that intangible something that orchestrates all of nature to the universal mission. The cosmic interpretation of creation. The..*

My imagination runs rampant on shrooms. Psychedelics have a tendency to explode in my mind bringing insight to me in fragments, jagged, mental shards.

I pull my notepad from my back pocket and begin scribbling wildly, thoughts entering my head, lingering for a moment and then darting off, daring me to pursue them....I wonder if all writers feel like me, like their channeling the greatest thinkers and writers in history, swimming in the pool of humanity with the big dogs, the intellectual sharks. It's like the words are coming through me, part Burroughs, part Thoreau, part Twain. Imagine being in touch with the soul of Mark Twain and having the ability to forward his thoughts on modern society. How would he feel about the Internet? About AIDS? About music and raving? Danny Boyle, Retro Beatnik Channeler.

Unfortunately, the flow is interrupted by the sound of more laughing, but now coming from the direction of the house. Propping myself up with my elbows, I see that the boys have decided to push things a bit, all of them standing just outside the circle of light being tossed across the field by Townsend's flood lamps.

Over the whir in my mind, I can just barely hear his Collie's hollow bark from the front porch..why me?..thud, the smack and the whomp are followed by battle cries as the guys pummel the side of the house with fresh crap and Mr. Townsend appears on his porch with his own battle cry, something to the effect of "good for nothing", blah, blah, "stinkin kids", blah, "kill all"..kill? The sound of a shotgun being fired lifts me to my feet. Townsend isn't chasing the guys, just standing in his yard firing his shotgun into the air, but they don't know that. As they run wildly in my direction, I notice that Poo is very animated, ducking, zigging and zagging, like bullets are raining down on him, like he's having some kind of traumatic wartime flashback. "Run Danny," he screams in horror, "Run!"

I fall into a jog behind the guys as they pass me. They continue to run as if their lives depend on it. Poo is sprinting like Carl Lewis with a hangover, then he goes down, face first into a big pile of dung. Maybe it's not boys and shit. Maybe it's just Poo and shit. It seems to be an ongoing theme for him. I grab him under his arm and hoist him up as he flails at the shit on his face.

Chad and Trav hurdle the fence in one stride, while Poo and I bring up the rear, a bit slower. On the other side, we collapse on the ground with a bad case of the giggles. Everyone laughs but Chad. He lies several yards away, clutching his ankle in obvious pain. "Chad, you all right bro?" "Does it look like I'm all right?," he snaps.

Poo pulls a fat splief out of his front pocket, places it between his teeth, lights it and hands it to Chad. "You'll be fine."

We decide to continue down the trail for a distance, Chad bringing up the rear with a slight limp. The joint makes it's rounds, but I pass. It burns out in Poo's mouth and he swallows the roach.

Eventually, the trail leads to a narrow, foot bridge that crosses to a tiny island in the middle of the Mill Creek...the bridge is shaky, basically just a series of two by fours with chains on either side for support, a bit of a balancing act, but everyone makes it across unscathed.

This island is one of my favorite places to come when I want to be alone and think. It's quiet, isolated, earthy. As

Trav fires up another joint, I crash out on my back once again and let the shrooms take me away.

It's been eons since I just laid and stared at the stars in the sky. My mother used to help me pick out the constellations, the north star, the big dipper...I was her "little dipper." I mourn the loss of such simplicity.

It occurs to me that this is the most rational thought I have had in several weeks, and I instantly begin to retrace my steps. When the flow checks in like this, I have to think..how was I able to conceive such a thought? At the same time, I meditate on the trappings of rational thought and the concept as a whole.

It seems that rational thought walks a path to choice, branching off in a number of other paths equal to one's amount of choices.

I begin to sketch a pool in my mind, and find myself wading in the shallow end of optimism, a million points of light in the sky above, shining down on me. I am nude and the water is cold, hugging my body tightly. My feet touch the bottom here, but in fairness I decide to test the deeper waters of pessimism.

Walking slowly and weightlessly, I make my way toward the far end. Soon I cannot touch the bottom and I slip under. The lights are distant now and my perspective shifts. How many more like-size points of darkness exist within the cracks? Several million, or very few? Only now can I make a rational decision on which path to take....so attitude, perspective and any number of biases challenge the flow, backing it up until the path is washed out and the way is unclear. *But how do I step outside that chain of remembering and forgetting that leads to bias?*

"Dan, you gonna hit this or what?"

"Huh?," I say, dazed.

"Last chance," says Chad, offering me the joint.

"No," I say. "No...I'm fine"

I lay my head back down—the sound of water rushing over the rocks nearby caresses my brain. Comfort visits my mind and body like a long lost friend inviting me to sleep over. I accept.

15

Several hours later the world comes hurtling back into view, sunlight pecking its way through the clouds in the morning sky. The guys lay to either side of me like slain soldiers crippled by mortar fire. Poo is still sporting a streak of shit from his left eye to his ear, his nose all scrunched up like he's been catching whiffs of it all night. Several empty bags litter the area..all the shrooms are history...every last one.

I might as well be a hundred years old. Every joint in my body aches, throbs, my right eye won't stop twitching, I can't move my legs and my breathing is labored, like I've been a 2 pack a day smoker for every one of those hundred years. Being a junkie must really suck. I promise myself never to let that happen. I hope it's not too late. Nah, this is just one big party. I'm going away to college in a couple of days. I owe this to myself.

My domestic side screams out, *owe it to yourself?, dammit Danny, couldn't you take yourself shopping or something?* What else do they call that?..superego, I think...id, ego, superego; anyway, maybe it's right. After all, I do need a new pair of shoes.

The sun is slowly eating up the shade from the trees that ring the field. It's going to be a hot one, I can feel it. No more drugs; today at least. *Screw you*, shouts the id, *more, more..shoes, Danny, shoes*, comes the calming voice of reason...*yeah, buy shoes, running shoes, to run and get more drugs*, pleads the id. *I don't think so*, chides the other side. I shake my head and send the squabbling brats toppling over in my mind. Ego tells them both to chill and puts them in front of the blackboard.

I will not bother Danny.
I will not bother Danny.
I will not both...they write.

Ahh..much better. I still can't feel my legs, but at least it's quiet, except for the birds and the river. A melodious calm washes over me as I sit and lazily watch the sunrise, listening to the birds sing. Music to my ears. Nature's techno. It can be heard on the waves crashing into a beach anywhere in the world, like now, in the rustling of the grass as the wind blows. All this bingeing and I've taken less and less time to enjoy the simpler things in life.

Travis is awake now. He stands up and walks quietly towards me, stepping just clear of Poo's head.

"Whatcha thinkin' about?," he questions, taking a seat on the ground.

"It's kinda heavy," I warn.

"I'll take my chances," he persists.

"I think all this druggin' is starting to get to me."

"Yeah, me too. I was thinking about that the other day myself."

"I can't figure out what the draw is. I really felt like I was on the verge of some sort of understanding last night..but, I don't know....it just continues to elude me."

"I hear ya."

"It's not really even that much fun anymore. I mean, look at us." Poo snores loudly on cue.

We both laugh as my solemn line of inquiry into our motivations dies an untimely death. I've been wanting to talk to Trav about the other night and the uneasy silence suggests that's he's been waiting for me to bring it up. "Trav, about the other night, I-"

"It's cool bro."

"I know..I mean, yeah, it's cool," I say, stammering a bit.

"It's no big deal."

"Yeah, we were all fucked up huh?"

"I wasn't that fucked up Dan."

"You weren't?"

"Well, I was, but that had nothing to do with it."

"With what?"

"With what we're talking about."

"Oh, right."

I always knew that when it came time to talk about the other night and my feelings for Travis, the words would come slowly, awkwardly. Is he trying to say that the kiss, now known only as *it*, meant more to him, or just that he's cool with it, fucked up or not?

"So it would have happened even if you hadn't been fucked up?," I ask. "Yeah. You?"

"Yeah," I say, smiling.

The smile he returns me answers my question, filling my head with a hundred more. Has he always felt this way? Has he ever been with a guy before? Would pursuing things ruin our friendship? What now?

"Two more days kiddo. You and me against the world. You ready?" I ask, changing the subject abruptly.

"Ready as I'll ever be," Trav admits.

"Higher learning. The pursuit of excellence. Academia."

"Term papers. Cramming for finals. All-nighters."

"Fuck that. We just have to find new ways to cheat...man, I gotta get with my mom about my schedule. You decided what you're takin' this semester?," I ask.

"Not really. It's all general ed for the first year or so anyway."
"Yeah, but I'd kind of like to get a head start on a major, ya know?"
"You got plenty of time to think about that."
"Yeah, I guess."
I really have no idea what I want to do with my life. College is a way of buying time more than anything else...English maybe, Journalism? I can't help but think that a degree is nothing more than a piece of paper though. I mean, I wipe my ass with paper, but I wouldn't wait four years in line to buy some.
"You still thinkin' about law school?," I ask.
"We'll see what happens. I'll take a couple law classes and see how I like it. I really don't know if I can afford it," he says, eyes narrowing as he looks out across the field. "Mom's gonna help me as much as she can, but business is slow."
Travis' mother owns a small Christian bookstore in town. His parents got divorced several months ago. "No help from pops?," I ask.
"No. Haven't even heard from him actually."
"I'm sorry."
"Don't be. He's a bastard," he says, yanking a piece of grass out of the ground.
"How's your mom taking it?"
"Really bad, you know she's like a totally devout Catholic.."
"She's guilt trippin', huh?"
"Yeah..the church doesn't look too kindly on divorce. And then there's me, her son," he says, turning to look at me.
"Her son, the hell-raiser?"
"Hell-raiser and fag," he finishes, leaning over and kissing me softly on the lips....my heart skips a beat, really, I totally missed a beat. I never pictured things happening like this.
"Old McDonald had a farm. E-I-E-I-O. And on that farm he had some shrooms. E-I-E-I-O. Here a shroom, there a shroom, everywhere a shroom, shroom..."

There's sort of this diseased irony that plagues my life; not true irony, but that Alanis Morissette type of irony, like nothing goes my way, like rain on my wedding day. God, I hate that song...anyway, imagine my life as a beautiful, serene lake with a thick layer of algae and slime on the surface and Jason is the Swamp Thing, rising slowly from the muck, destroying my moment forever. Staggering a couple of steps in our direction, he stops and tries to focus. "Well, gooooood morning Vietnam!"

The outburst wakes everyone with a start. As Jason gets closer, I can see the bandage on his face. It looks like he'll be marked from his right ear down and across to his bottom lip. He has a jug of what looks like orange juice in one hand and a bottle of prescription pills in the other. He stops, washes a couple down and continues walking.

Pain killers.

An all time favorite with the crew.

This can't be happening. My world is going to be a wash for another 24 hours. Not even the mighty superego can resist codeine-induced bliss. Id begins scribbling madly on the board...

Danny will do drugs.

Danny will do drugs.

Danny will do..

Jason's a mess. He starts singing again.

"Here comes the sun. Little darlin. Here comes the sun. It's all right. Do-do do," plopping down near Travis and surveying the scene, a devilish smile tugging on his stitched lip. "Thought I might find you freaks out here."

Grunts all the way around.

"Party on," he says as he begins rationing out the rest of the pills.

Everyone partakes except for Chad.

"I have to get us home in a bit fellas. I can't be driv...son of a bitch."

"Wassup dude?," I ask.

"Tell me I'm wrong and I didn't leave my car parked in the center of the frickin' road last night. Somebody, please. Please? Tell me I am fucking wrong."

"You're *fucking* wrong? Who's wrong? You mean Wong, that slanty eyed bitch you fucke-," starts Poo.

In the blink of an eye, Chad is all over him, yanking him up from the ground by the collar of his shirt. One hand jammed in a belt loop on the back of his jeans, the other placed firmly on his neck to steer, Chad rushes Poo down to the creek and tosses him in head first. He flounders for a moment and then plants his feet in the creek bed, standing up straight and pulling himself onto dry ground, dropping there, his feet still dangling in the current. Without saying a word, Chad spits in his direction and walks back toward us, wiping his hands together, "I've always wanted to do that. Damn, that felt good."

It takes us all a minute to process what just happened. A delayed reaction. In unison, we all bust out laughing hysterically at Chad's work.

"He needed a bath anyway, the little shit."

"Fuck you," shouts Poo halfheartedly at the sky, causing us to laugh even harder. "What'd you have to fuckin' do that for?" More laughter.

"You stink. Wash that crap off your face you frickin' dirtbag."

We all seem almost immediately intoxicated by the downers, probably because none of us has eaten since yesterday, unless you count the shrooms. Some diet. Beer and shrooms. And downers, the breakfast of champions..*woo-hoo...we're cookin' now baby, ain't nothin' stoppin' this train.*

I'm alarmed at my sarcasm....I can picture her in my head, my sarcasm that is, a bag lady, her pantyhose full of holes, her face riddled with warts and her hair looking like it hasn't been washed in years. She's pushing a shopping cart full of emotional baggage that has my name written on it in big, bold, Road Runner and Wild Coyote ACME lettering, repeating in her tired, emphysema-havin', toothless voice, *ain't no stoppin' this train*. Swatting flies away from her haggard head, she stops for a moment and then continues on..*no sirree, not this train*.

Could this really be happening to me? My dad always warned me that sarcasm could be a sign of an impending bout of cynicism, the same kind of cynicism that crippled him in his later years, sapped him of desire, ruined his good-hearted nature, robbed him of motivation. I have always thought of sarcasm as a kind of defense mechanism to help me deal with the twisted nature of the world around me. Cynicism could be used the same way I suppose, arising from sarcasm pushed to the limit, put to the test, placed on trial. New and Improved Sarcasm. More dangerous. More self-destructive.

Jason and Poo have discovered more shrooms on the other side of the bridge. I can hear them shouting. Madness. I'm starting to get a really bad feeling about all of this.

"You think my car got towed Dan?," asks Chad as we navigate the bridge.

"I hate to be a buzzkill bro, but I'm almost sure that your car's been towed. You left it right in the middle of the road. What were you thinkin' anyway?"

"Me? Am I the only one responsible for thinking around here? I wasn't thinking. That's the problem Danny. None of us are thinking. This is fucked up. I mean look at 'em."

With the last bit of orange juice, Jason washes down a whole handful of mushroom caps, as Poo waits patiently for his turn. Leaving a mouthful, Jason passes the jug. Travis stands by and laughs uneasily, shaking his head in disbelief as Poo swallows a handful of his own and chases them with OJ.

"You guys are nuts," announces Chad. "You know how fucked you guys are gonna be? We've got a long walk ahead of us."

"It's your car bro. *You* have a long walk. We'll be here when you get back," says Poo, fully aware that he's crossing the line.

I grab Chad around the waist as he lunges at Poo, but his left fist still connects with a thud. Poo stumbles backwards, dazed, bleeding from his nose, while I struggle to keep Chad from breaking free. Travis steps in between the two, shielding Chad as Poo regains his composure and makes a move.. "What the fuck was that for?"

"For being an asshole," shouts Chad angrily, still trying to worm his way out of my hands.

Travis moves forward and places his hands lightly on Poo's shoulders in an attempt to keep him from getting any closer. "Get your hands off me Trav," shrugging his shoulders. "I'm chill. Talk to crazy man over there."

"You haven't seen crazy yet."

"Oh yeah, why don't you show me crazy Chad. Mr. fuckin' tough guy. Mr. all-Ameri-"

A searing pain in my stomach. Chad's elbow lands solidly in my gut and drops me to my knees as he rushes at Poo. A right hook takes him down this time. Damn, Chad's devastating with both fists - I file that away, reminding myself never to pick a fight with him. He fights dirty too, kicking Poo repeatedly in the stomach. Eyes still watering from the elbow, I see Travis finally tackle him squarely and wrestle him to the ground.

"Chill the fuck out," the threat echoes around the field.

It is so rare to see Travis get upset. I know he's not bluffing though. Isn't the most mild-mannered, quiet one in the group always the biggest bad ass when push comes to shove?

Travis' dad, a Vietnam vet, showed him how to box when he was younger - schoolyard skills. I think I'm probably the only one of us who knows about it. He doesn't really like people to know, afraid that he'll constantly be called on to prove himself. Chad is so taken by surprise that he's speechless..matter of fact, no one says a word or even moves for what seems like an eternity until Poo, lying in a fetal position grasping his stomach, begins moaning loudly. Jason slowly walks to his side and crouches down.

"What the fuck is wrong with you guys?," I plead from a distance.

Chad slaps his forehead and slumps backwards into the grass, as if just now realizing the gravity of what he's done. "Chad, you got any of those bags left?," inquires Travis.

Poo is hyper-ventilating. Chad silently reaches into his pocket and tosses Travis the last bag who places it over Poo's mouth and tells him to breathe. "Slower, bro. Slower." It's getting hot. Very hot.

16

Chad's car is nowhere to be found. On the way down the trail, he remembered leaving his keys in the ignition, so it could just as easily have been stolen as towed. Either way, we don't have much of a choice except to walk.

Poo and Jason are tripping out, Chad is furious with himself, I'm exhausted, and Travis is trying to hold us all together. My body is calling me names again. I can feel the effects of dehydration coming on. "We're going to have to find a phone fellas. There's no way I'm making it back into town."

"Yeah, I don't feel so hot myself," mumbles Poo, wiping his brow.

"Join the club," adds Chad. "My car," he mumbles to himself.

I've been watching Jason. If anybody is seriously overdue for some time in detox, it's Jason. He can't even put one foot in front of the other, like he's mesmerized by the steam rising off the road, trying to step over it, tripping on it and stumbling, almost going down, like he's in some kind of hallucinogenic stupor, climbing an imaginary staircase and missing

133

every other step.

"J, you all right bro?"

No response.

"Yo, Jason, you all right?," I repeat louder.

He nods, but doesn't say anything. A car appears over the dip in the road ahead of us and flies by as Chad makes a halfhearted attempt to extend his thumb.

"Asshole," he screams, almost as an afterthought.

A second car, just moments later, startles Jason and he stumbles, falling to the ground on his elbows and face. As I rush over to help him, I notice his bandage has come loose. The area around the stitches on his faces has begun to swell, maybe from the heat, maybe infection, and now the bandage is useless, covered with dirt and gravel from the roadside. He sits helpless, gazing off into outer space, gently touching the skin around the cut. "You're not all right, are ya kid?"

This time he shakes his head and promptly begins swatting at imaginary bugs, snapping at them with his mouth, his teeth clacking together with every bite. Then he realizes it's just the bandage dangling from his face and he tears it off, hardly cringing at the pain. "Danny, I wanna go home. Please," he pleads uncharacteristically.

"Come on Jason. We're not getting any closer with you sittin' there on your tired, trippin' ass," interjects Chad from the sidelines, clearly agitated.

"What's the hell's gotten into you, Chad?," asks Travis.

"Fuck him," I say under my breath, turning back to Jason.

"Yeah, well fuck you too Danny. Fuck you," he hollers, walking ahead and raising his middle finger in the air.

Jason's sitting with his arms wrapped around his legs now, rocking back and forth, a tear rolling down his bruised face. I'm suddenly stricken with empathy and compassion, not just for Jason, but for all of us, for letting the drugs get the better of us, come between us. For the first time in several hours, I'm able to make a connection with Jason.

Wiping the tear from his eye, he nods, as if to say he feels the same way and without saying a word, he also says he's sorry. I grab him by the back of his neck and plant a kiss on his forehead, then help him to his feet. As he brushes himself off, Poo walks up.

"I'm tweakin' guys. I shouldn't have ate those shrooms, uh-huh...bad call, *real* bad call..I can't see, the sun, I'm seein' spots. You guys see 'em?," he babbles, covering his right eye with his hand and opening and closing his left eye.

"Come on guys. Let's catch up to Chad," suggests Travis, ignoring Poo's ramblings.

Chad hasn't covered that much ground...about a hundred yards. As we get closer, he turns to look at us and points into the distance. Cupping my eyes from the sun, I spot a house on the horizon, about a mile or so down the road....Poo is totally wigging out, rubbing his eyes, swearing that they're disintegrating. I suppose under different circumstances I might find it amusing, but right now, it's just annoying.

"None of you guys give a shit that I can't see? You think there's a hospital nearby?"

"Would you shut up?," I ask. "Think anybody's home?," Chad asks as we get closer.

There's a truck parked in the driveway, but other than that, no sign that anyone might be home. Chad plods fearlessly ahead again, leading us right up to the front door and knocking loudly, then anxiously ringing the bell. Four times.

"Chill, they're gonna think we're freaks."

"Would they be wrong?," he states with a straight face.

"No, but it might make the difference between help or no help."

"I vote help," chirps Poo. "We need help guys. Seriously."

We all try to contain our laughter at Poo's condition, seems like the mood has lightened a bit, but there's no answer at the door. "We might have to break in," Chad mentions casually.

"Break in, are you crazy?," I freak, admittedly overacting a bit, hoping he's not serious.

"There's nobody here dude. We just throw up a window, use the phone and jet. They live in the middle of frickin' nowhere, ya think they lock their doors and windows?," asks Chad, striding around to the side of the house and opening the first window he comes to with no difficulty. After looking in both directions, he places his hands on the windowsill and skillfully lifts himself inside.

"You've done this before, haven't you?," I joke.

"Actually, yeah," he replies, fussing with the drapes before shutting the window and making his move.

He opens the front door and motions us in, as a butler would, with a bow. The interior of the house oozes with testosterone. A rifle rack in the entry hall? Come on. Hello, welcome to our armory. A deer's head sits mounted over the fireplace in the living room. The more I look, I notice the subtle female touches. It's tidy. Clean.

"I'll be in the bathroom guys," says Jason, in a barely audible voice.

Poo disappears upstairs immediately, with a criminal's haste. For a moment it occurs to me that he might try to rob the place, but I pretend I didn't hear myself...my suspicions are temporarily put to rest when he reappears on the balcony with a pair of underpants on his head. "Mmm..I can smell mama bear's trim," he says, giggling like a ten year old.

Chad heads straight for the phone in the kitchen as Travis and I pace nervously in front of the window, surveying the front yard for signs of life.

"Jason, you gonna be long?," I holler down the back hallway. No response.

"What's up bro?," Trav asks.

"I have to take a leak," I explain, pacing faster. "Check in the living room."

There's a small bathroom set just off the laundry room on the first level. As I shut the door, Travis squeezes in quickly behind me, locking it and falling against it.

"I was-," I start to say, but then our eyes meet and I forget what I was going to say. "Hey," he says shyly.

"What's up?," I ask, even though I know.

I feel like I'm staring right through him; I might as well be staring at my reflection, we are so much alike and have wanted the same thing for so long, and you know what comes next, that smile, except this time it means even more, and it's a hundred times sexier, which I never thought possible. "Not much," he says nonchalantly.

We both hesitate to say anything else, savoring the anticipation, dining on it even, cleaning our plates.

"We didn't get a chance to finish our conversation earlier."

"We keep missing each other," I add agreeably.

There's a loud noise upstairs, like maybe Poo's jumping on the bed. We both look at the ceiling and laugh, then our eyes meet.

"You know I was so jealous the other night...of Kelly," I say.

"She wasn't that good, if it means anything to you."

"Yeah..but you were."

The sexual tension is so thick we could slice it up and make hormone sandwiches. "I try," he says modestly.

Suddenly we're all over each other, kissing each other's necks, lips and ears, our hands playing over each other's bodies, but I stop him- "Travis, I..uh, shit, I'm really into this, but we can't, I mean-"

"I'm sorry Dan, I..I'm," he says, turning and reaching for the doorknob. "Travis," turning him around. "*I'm* sorry," I say.

"That sucks."

"What?," I ask defensively.

"It fucking sucks Danny, it fucking sucks that either one of us has to be *fucking* sorry," he says in frustration, running his fingers through his hair.

Trav's statement knocks the wind out of me. What the hell *am* I sorry about? I stare blankly at the wall, then at

Travis and his normally stoic demeanor collapses, pain all over his face. I grab him and hug him tightly. I've never seen Travis as affected by anything before. I'm surprised and touched. Deeply touched.

"It's all right kiddo," rubbing his back. "I'm not going anywhere," I promise.

"I know Dan, I'm just sick of pretending."

"I know Trav, I know, I am too, but-"

"But what?," he says, pulling away, frustrated again.

"I..I don't know," and we lean in slower this time, kissing each other again.

"Damn, you got some timing," I say, laughing uneasily.

"I'm sorry bro, must be those pills that Jason gave me making me so emotional," he says smiling, turning the heat down on the moment.

We regard each other with affection and mutual respect for an extended moment, and then he walks out.

What am I doing?

Mass confusion mixed with overwhelming joy and a dash of terror, and then I realize I can't take a piss because I have a hard-on the size of North Dakota.

Back in the kitchen, Chad is busy trying to convince his brother to come pick us up. "You gotta do me this favor," he pleads.

I can only hear one side of the conversation, but I'm sure he's getting an earful. It's no secret that Chad's brother doesn't approve of his little brother's lifestyle choices. Steve's an athlete as well, and a good student, straight as an arrow.

"It's a long story...I'll tell ya later. Can you come get us? All you have to do is drive west on Old Harris. We're going to start walking again."

"Walking again? Can't we raid the fridge, turn on the tube and chill?," I ask Chad as he hangs up the phone.

17

There's suddenly a sound in the next room, like a sliding glass door being opened, rolling solidly on a track. Chad and I creep to the alcove and peer cautiously into the living room. A man. And a gun. And a sinking feeling, like the shit is about to hit the fan. Hard.

He's 50ish with graying hair, a prominent nose, fishing hat, down vest and knee high boots. He hangs his hat on the rack near the door, cradling a large hunting rifle with a scope in his free hand. Then Jason appears in the hallway, talking to himself, "Much better," he mumbles, a fresh bandaid on his face.

"Mary? Hun, you home?," with a thick Southern accent.

I'm panicked. Very bad in these types of situations. Have to think. There's a chance he might not use the gun on us if we give ourselves up. He's a hunter, not a killer right? Duh, isn't that what hunters do? Kill? Shit...we're fucked.

"That you Mary?," comes the voice from the back room again.

Jason is now standing in the threshold of the front door, waving us out, but we can't leave Poo. I point up, as if to tell him we have to warn Poo, but it's too late.

"Hey guys, there's enough cash up here to buy a car with. We can drive our own happy asses home," carries Poo's voice from the loft.

Their eyes lock and the owner of the house charges the stairs, a muted squeal of surprise leaping from Poo's mouth as he stumbles backwards into the bedroom. As the rest of us rush into the living room, the man tumbles back down the stairs, his rifle not far behind. Poo stands on the landing, one crazed eye visible through the leg of the panties still glued to his face, maniacally holding a golf club in his hands, his knuckles white on the grip, shaking uncontrollably.

"Greg, what the f-"

Racing down the stairs to finish the job, he beats the man mercilessly with the nine iron. I can hear his ribs breaking under the weight of the club. Poo's lost it.

"Greg, put it down."

"Stop it. You're gonna kill him."

"What the fuck?"

"Greg, don't-"

In the confusion, we all let loose at once, a bundle of frayed nerves, shouting at Poo, begging him to chill. When he starts coming down on the man's head, I have to act. Timing the blows, I step forward and catch the club on the upswing, yanking it out of his hands. The man lies unconscious, bleeding, at my feet.

"Danny, he was going to kill me," Poo bellows through a sudden torrent of tears, tearing the underwear from his head.

"Chill bro. Chill. I know. I know."

"Are you out of your mind?," shouts Chad angrily.

"Ah fuck. I killed him. I, ah shi-"

"You didn't kill him Greg, you jus-"

"Ah no. He had a gun Dan. He had a gun."

"Greg, calm down dude. Everything's gonna be all right."

I suddenly remember that Poo is tripping. It may take

him awhile to get over this little episode. A long while.

I check the man's pulse. It's weak, but it's there. Poo is bawling now. "I killed him. I know I did."

"He's alive Greg. He's alive. Chill."

"Yeah everything'll be just jim fuckin' dandy Dan. Breaking and entering, robbery, assault and battery," rages Chad melodramatically, his hand on his forehead ala Richard Lewis, pacing back and forth.

"Well why don't you help out instead of running your fucking mouth, Chad?"

"I'm calling 911," he says, heading for the kitchen.

"Just dial and hang up," I insist.

I can hear the phone clatter on the floor in the kitchen. Chad hastily makes his way back into the living room and joins us at the rear door. I stop for a moment to survey the scene one last time, making sure we aren't leaving anything behind and then slide the door shut.

We reach the wooded area behind the house fairly quickly. It's thick, but not dense enough to stop us. Chad leads, bolting into the woods leading us parallel to the road, the sound of sirens in the distance carrying softly through the trees...an open field ahead, no path that sticks to the cover. "On the road again boys," determines Chad.

As we emerge from the woods, I look west towards the house. There's an ambulance, two police cars and a fire department vehicle of some sort parked on the property, several men walking quickly across the lawn to the front door.

The rest of the guys are strutting ahead without me, in a very deliberate cadence, refusing to look back. "Come on Dan, don't draw attention," orders Chad.

I break into a jog and catch up, walking beside them, trying my hardest to look innocent. Casual. *Hey, how's it goin?..Oh yeah, great..cool..just chillin' here. Yeah, just gettin' some exercise...nice day for a walk..chillin'..don't mind us..just mindin' our own business..don't know nothin' about that guy that just got beaten half to death down the road..no sirree..not a clue*..it isn't working very well, we all look guilty as sin.

After walking in silence for about a half mile, Steve's red Jeep Cherokee appears. Chad waves him down and we all pile in, trying to disguise our sense of urgency.

"Wow, thanks bro, you're a life saver," says Chad, almost quaintly.

"No problem kid. You guys all right? An ambulance raced by me not too far back and I got kinda worried."

Poo looks agitated, constipated almost, his face frozen, like his brain has locked up, his memory stuck in the moment the club landed. As the moment plays back in his head, his face twitches, his body shudders with each blow. I nudge him with my elbow, breaking the trance.

"Yeah, we saw it too. Not for us though."

Steve nods as he leans on the steering wheel and pulls a three point turn in the middle of the road, gunning the engine, heading east, and sending Jason toppling over in the back. From behind the seat, he graciously extends his middle finger, rubbing his head with contempt.

"Does anybody have any drugs on them?," Steve begins the interrogation.

Or weapons, I think to myself. What is this, *customs*?

The crew ignores him. I can't believe Chad told him about the shrooms, and why did he have to call his brother of all people? - we've all ready beaten each other up enough this week about the drugs.

In the front seat, Steve goes after Chad about his job. Apparently his employers have been in touch.

"You weren't huffin' gas or anything?"

"I wasn't huffin' gas Steve. We just did a little nitrous."

"Nitrous oxide *gas* Chad. It's semantics. They said you were smokin' marijuana inside the store too."

Eek..I hate the word marijuana. It sounds so sterile.

Suddenly I feel like I'm in a *really bad* ABC after school special, like all this drama is being staged to peddle Nestle's Quik to latchkey kids; processed even, like Cheese Whiz, or Spam. It's an extremely unsettling sensation.

"Yeah, we were. I was tryin' to come down off the *coke* I was doin' all night."

"Coke?"

"Yeah, I needed a boost when the *ecstasy* wore off."

"You were doing ecstasy?"

"Yeah," answers Chad angrily. "I got some coke left. You want some?," screams Chad, pulling a vial out of his pocket.

He proceeds to load the bullet at the top of the vial with a bump and jam it up his nose, snorting loudly, loading it again and hitting his other nostril as Steve reaches over and tries to grab it, the Jeep veering off the left side of the road as they struggle. Regaining control, he slams on the brakes, sending Jason over the top of the back seat, right onto Travis's lap.

"I'll kill your ass my damn self," Jason screams, throwing himself at Steve in the driver's seat.

The situation quickly escalates as Steve jumps out of the Jeep, narrowly escaping Jason's outstretched arms aimed at his neck, and slams the door on the top of his head. Circling around the front, he reaches out to open the passenger side door. Chad swings the door open solidly into his chest, knocking him to the ground in a cloud of dust.

Steve tackles his brother as he steps out, the two sprawling out on the ground by the roadside. For a moment they just wrestle, neither one committing themselves to a brawl, then Chad starts slapping him. Using his weight to his advantage, Steve grabs Chad's hands and throws him off balance, rolling over on top of him.

Jason is the first to act, climbing out the open door on the driver's side and rushing around to the melee. With a running start, he kicks the side of Steve's head with the bottom of his foot, following him as he falls away, kicking him repeatedly in the side of the head.

"Ass," kick. "Hole," kick.

"Ass," kick. "Fuck," kick.

"Jason," shouts Travis, clambering to get out.

"Son of a fucking bitch," stomp, stomp.

Travis grabs Jason roughly, pinning his arms to his side and pulling him away, his foot landing one last time. Something tells me that there would be no stopping Jason if he really wanted to finish up...instead he stands back voluntarily, fists clenched, scowling, stitches straining over taut muscles. Chad stands up and lurches unsteadily toward his brother. "Now what's up bitch? Huh?," he yells.

Poo and I are the last to get out, both of us a bit stunned by the drama. Steve looks hurt, but he's not unconscious, possibly even spared of any broken bones. He stands up slowly, grabbing his baseball cap off the ground and brushing it off; a great deal of self-control, considering the situation. He fixes a stare on Chad..*your own fucking brother, look what you've become, how dare you, you selfish, spoiled little druggie, you better open your eyes, first your job, your car, now me, how much can you lose before you wake the fuck up?*

Chad's gaze remains stern, refusing to bend to his brother's nonverbal plea, the cocaine pelting his brain, his heart racing. *I care, that's why I give you a hard time, this is the thanks I get? I've been nothing but good to you Chad...*

The gravity of the moment brings weight to everyone's stance, except for Chad's. Shoulders sag, heads drop, victory for none, defeat for all. Chad was way out of line.

We stand in silence as Steve deliberately strides around to the front of the Jeep, opens the door, pulls it shut softly and starts the ignition, revving the engine and then driving off.

"No shit," mutters Poo in disbelief.

"Thanks guys," says Chad, brushing himself off.

"For what?," I ask.

"For backing me up," he says matter of factly.

"Who backed you up?...why the fuck do you always have to be one up on everybody Chad?," I shout, catching the guys off guard.

"Who am I trying to get one up on? My brother? That piece of shit was trying to get over on me. Fuck him," he says angrily, sneering at me.

"He's your brother Chad. He's *family*. He might have a weird way of showing it but he cares about you."

"You don't know him Dan. And you don't know shit about *us*," putting his finger in my face.

"Fuck it," I say turning around. "It's not worth it."

Last month in Biology class we were taught that human beings only use a small percentage of their brain.

I wonder what percentage of our hearts we use? And why do we make the choice to hate? To fight? Ego? Foolish pride?

18
5:00 pm, Tuesday evening

It's amazing to me that we've all remained friends for as long as we have. If it's not me and Chad, it's Greg and Chad, or me and Jason...we're constantly at each other's throats lately, acting out like punks.

Chad walks silently next to me. Our eyes meet and he hangs his head. "Can I just give you a blanket apology now, for any trash I've talked in the past, or ever will talk? I don't mean it, bro. Seriously. I know I'm hot-headed...." I nod in silent acceptance, though I wonder if Chad will ever learn to take responsibility for the way he acts.

We ultimately decide to hide out, at least until it gets dark. Jason has a joint to smoke. It's big enough to take the edge off, so you know it's pretty damn big.

Soft pine needles blanket the shaded ground, shielded from the sun by the interweaving of the branches overhead. As the joint goes around, Jason stands and steps off to the side, rhyming to himself under his breath..

Times are changin', rearrangin', everybody's gaugin,

now the streets are deadly, my flow is steady, rhymin's what I do and the beats are what lead me, to this occupation, a revelation, that I could rock a mic and be causin' devastation, day and night and night and day, yet I stay low key and live life my way, and if I stray, let what's done be done, cuz only suckers hide and only suckers run, while this MC rides, and yes I am the one and only MC who will not be faded, by the madness created, in life, is it a game of chance? nah, we're all victims of circumstance

"Right on bro," Trav praises, clapping loudly. Jason smiles.

"J, why don't you do something with that?," asks Travis.

"What, my rhymes? Like what?"

"I don't know. Maybe you could give Vanilla Ice a run for his money or something."

"Very funny."

"Seriously bro. I mean, not the Vanilla Ice shit, but you should flex those skills somewhere. Maybe find somebody who spins breakbeats and collaborate on something."

"Nah."

"Why not?"

I can see where Travis is going with all of this, but pep talks often get taken as criticism by Jason, rather than sincere encouragement. Jason doesn't like to think anybody's telling him what to do or how to live.

"Cuz it's my own thing. I don't got nothin' to prove."

"No, I just say that because your shit's good. And you obviously enjoy it."

"Yeah."

"You wouldn't necessarily have to perform. I know most white rap artists don't get much respect. Record companies and publishers pay good money for writing talent though."

Is it any wonder why I adore Travis? He doesn't say much, but when he does speak, it's always with purpose. Too many people in this world are in love with the sound of their own voices, talking all the time, but not saying a thing.

"Like you don't have to be the next Vanilla Ice, just write the next "Ice, Ice Baby", know what I'm sayin'?," Trav says, chuckling.

"Right. I don't know. Maybe."

A 'maybe' is more than I've gotten out of Jason in all the years we've been friends. 'Maybe' is monumental.

"O.K., we've got Jason's future figured out. Now how 'bout the rest of us?," I say, clapping my hands together loudly.

"I'm scared," admits Poo. "I don't know what I'm going to do. All I *know* is kickin' it with you guys. Rollin' joints. Dancin'. Buggin' out."

"I'm with you there bro," says Chad. "Well, 'cept for the rollin' joints. I never could roll a fucking joint," he says, drawing a laugh from everybody.

"You still lookin' at getting your AA degree?," asks Trav.

"I don't know...I'll probably end up at junior college in the fall. I can live at home and stuff that way, just wish there was something I was good at, Jason writes rhymes, Dan, you're always scribbling in that journal..not that anybody's ever seen it, but I'm sure you're a talented writer too. Trav, you're just flat out a brain, you can do whatever you want. And Poo, well," Chad says, putting his arm around Greg, "O.K. so misery loves company."

"You're forgetting one thing," insists Travis.

"What's that? Ice cream?," Chad says limply.

"Close. You *sell* ice cream right. And what else?"

"Huh?"

"What else do you sell?"

"Oh thanks bro. I'll just deal drugs for the rest of my life. I'll be on the corner if you need me."

"No, not drugs. Anything but. Why not sales, marketing, something like that?"

"Dude, I'm not sitting around with a bunch of suits all day long kickin' it about dish soap and shit like that."

"Chad, how many times have you talked someone into that

last pill whether they needed it or not?"

"Uh.."

"Or introduced a someone to nitrous and fully sold 'em on it?"

"More than I care to count."

"Well the field's wide open bro. Advertising even. Record promotion. Club promotion. We even have the contacts for that built right in around here."

I'm starting to get inspired sitting here listening to Travis. Maybe I can stay close to the underground too. Write for a 'zine or something. Musical criticism. Party reviews. Artist interviews. "What about you Greg? There's got to be something you're good at, something you enjoy."

"Not really. Unless I start a joint rolling service or something like that."

"I'll be your first customer," jokes Chad.

"I'm thinking about moving back to New York actually and working for my uncle at his insurance company. I don't know jack shit about the biz, but he said he'd teach me. Would you buy insurance from *me* though? *I* wouldn't even buy insurance from me."

Laughter. The sweetest music of all. Was it Jimmy Buffett who said that if we couldn't laugh we would all go insane? What a wise, wise man.

The sun is starting to go down. Streaks of pink and orange color the clouds in the sky haphazardly, like strokes from a cosmic child's crayon. For the next half hour or so, we sit solemnly, side by side, watching the sunset, allowing our cares and worries to set with it, indifferent to the meaning of life and the nature of the universe, untouchable, yet scarred, above it, yet down in it - "Well boys, I guess this is it," I notice quietly.

"Yeah, I guess so," mourns Chad.

"I'm gonna miss you guys, seriously. I couldn't imagine having better friends."

"Yeah, it's been quite a ride," says Jason, reminiscing.

"Yes, yes..," says Poo.

"I don't want you guys to hesitate to call if you ever need anything, even just to talk. And I'm sure I speak for Travis *and* myself when I say that the door's always open if you want to come visit," as Travis nods his head.

"Why you talkin all this good-bye stuff Dan? We still got a couple days left together. Don't start gettin' heavy."

"Well, we might not get any more time alone like this. It's as good a time as any. I guess none of us really know what to expect..but for what it's worth...I'd like you guys to know that I'll always be here if you need me."

"Damn Dan," says Poo, wiping a tear out of his eye.

"Shit, we've all been cryin' like bitches all week," says Jason, looking away.

It's difficult when friends collectively reach an intersection in their lives. Some will walk the same road as your own, so that you need not walk alone. To those who you must bid farewell, you can only hope that the road they must walk isn't dark, but well lit, and hold fast the possibility that your paths will cross again. When they get lost, you can offer them a map. And when it comes time for you to move ahead, you can offer them a ride.

"Tell you what, we're all going to be just fine," I predict optimistically.

"Yeah, I think so," agrees Chad.

"Hellz yeah we're gonna be all right," shouts Jason. "The crew's charmed. You can't touch us."

"If we were charmed there'd be a stretch caddy rollin' up right about now," says Poo. "Damn. No shit. We gotta long walk huh?"

"Right, and I have a lot to do tomorrow," I say.

"Let's do this then," agrees Trav, standing up and brushing himself off.

Hardly a word is said on the trek into town. Not an uneasy silence. It just seems that it's all been said, at one time or another.

19

I awake on the couch at my place, late Wednesday morning. My mother has already come home for the night, slept and left for work..luckily she thought to stretch a blanket out over me. My stomach's rumbling like I haven't eaten in days. Actually I haven't, and I can hear my mom's voice in my head, the concern, the love.

I cringe. It's such a pitiful statement on the status of my priorities. It wouldn't have made sense to interrupt my bingeing these last few days with a meal now would it?

After dragging myself up from the couch, I make breakfast, trying to take my time to enjoy the process for once. The process of cooking for myself feels cleansing. Nourishment. Real food. Eggs, bacon, toast with extra butter and jelly, a tall glass of milk doing my body good..I had forgotten what eggs even taste like, it's been so long since I actually bothered to notice.

I sit for a long time at the kitchen table staring out the window at the sun. In a distant corner of my mind, I'm hoping that a renegade ray of sunshine will deliver mundanity to my doorstep. I never thought I'd feel that way, but I do, sentimental almost, like I just want to love, and be loved, and see the world through sober eyes for a change.

After eating, I decide to take a bath, reflect a bit and engage the flow. It's a bit of a ritual I have; Zen and the Art of Bathing—bubble bath, tea lights and a collection of subliminal beats to keep me company. Lately, it's been DJ Shadow providing the entertainment.

As I slide into the hot water, my mind goes under too, and I start thinking about everything, then nothing, then everything, no middle ground, point, counterpoint..Travis, identity, drugs, still such an enigma to me-

—I often tell myself I have no regrets about the years I've spent under influence. I've used drugs as a battering ram to break down mental walls, as a catalyst to creativity, a door to my subconscious and a window to my soul. They've brought a certain level of honesty to the relationship that I have with myself and exposed me to the world beyond the senses, to the bigger picture.

They've made me more self-aware, open-minded and worldly, even improved my sense of humor-I mean, how could anyone take life too seriously after experiencing Disney World on acid?.....isn't that all kind of romanticizing the "drug experience" though?

Lately I've been thinking that maybe I'm that same open-minded, self-aware, worldly person without the drugs? Maybe all the self-discovery that they seem to afford me is really just a natural part of the maturation process? Maybe drugs just aren't for me anymore?

I suppose it all comes down in the end to the roles that we play and the masks we wear...remembering Mom delivering a rather melodramatic monologue once on role-playing: "It's so hard to be good mother, a devoted wife, a secretary, a loving sister and daughter, and still have time for ME," goes the classically regarded line from the Pamela Boyle one woman

show.

At the time, I couldn't really relate. To me, mom was mom. Or mom *as* a secretary. Or mom *as* a sister. In any case, she was *always*, first and foremost, mom. I guess I never really considered how demanding the other roles may be, or that she might long to be someone other than mom on occasion. As I am called on to play more and varied roles, I have a whole new appreciation for Pamela Boyle, the person, first and foremost, human, just like you and me...Danny Boyle, Party Boy, comes easy to me. It's a part I know well, possibly too well, forsaking the rest of me, the understudies - Danny Boyle, Friend. Son. Student. Writer. Lover...and the word, back and forth in my head like a ping pong ball, bouncing higher, through the eye of a bottleneck in the flow, like it's all about to come me, and then it does—I am full-on, head over heels *in love*, with Travis.

I bolt upright in the bathtub, water splashing over the sides and across the floor. *In love with Travis?* I would later write this in my journal-

Azure fireballs erupt over a wind swept plain in my mind, sand peeling back in layers from the face of the looking glass, covered for so many years by the very elements of which it was shaped, mirrored, a fragmented reflection, chipped at the ends.

Just like that, it's all right there in front of me, my mouth agape, the flicker of the tea lights playing across the tile in the dark bathroom. It's hard to explain the rush that comes with such an epiphany, but it's a moment I won't soon forget, if ever.

At the altar of self, I found my religion.

All this time thinking it was the world that I was fighting and it has really been myself, scared, didn't want to accept Danny Boyle, Homosexual, the one role I was not only forsaking, but hiding from, running from. Could it be that simple? Well, it's certainly not simple. Sexuality is a pretty heavy concept. But could it be that obvious? I mean, I've always known I was different, but I've never been able to *accept it*. What a world of difference there is between the two, many worlds even.

No wonder I've been edgy, confused, hurting, and it fully explains the drugs, thinking it would all go away, trying to forget, and the acting out too, it all makes sense now. I thought denial and addiction were for people on Oprah, and here I am, a case study.

I stand slowly in the tub and then step out, walking to the mirror and staring silently at my reflection for several minutes. I pinch my cheeks, like I'm trying to make sure this isn't all coming to me in a dream. Then I smile, a weightless smile, with nothing on the fringes of my psyche to drag it down. Not even gravity can take this one away from me.

In the closet

Blue balls and
moth balls
keeping company with the greats
candy coated skeletons
ship of fools, my mates
bag of bones
I got enough of own
Don't ask
Don't tell
I'd rather rot in hell
you say I will
yet your just like me
can't see the forest for the trees
when you're down on your knees
Don't worry, big guy
I'll leave the door open
On my way out

20

I end up back in the bathtub, sitting silently for almost an hour, thinking about Travis, playing with myself and then falling asleep, awakened by loud voices at the front door. "Come in," I scream ahead, grabbing a towel and wrapping it around myself.

"Danster, you decent?," asks Chad jokingly through the open window, as Trav opens the door smiling, giving me the once-over with his eyes.

"Uh, decent? Yeah. Where's Poo?," I ask.

"He's way wigged out about yesterday bro," Jason informs me.

"You guys catch the news last night? We're home invaders."

"No shit, we were on T.V.?," asks Jason excitedly.

"Well, *we* weren't of course, but there was a blurb about the incident on the six o'clock news. The guy's in stable condition downtown," I explain.

"Maybe we should send flowers or something," says Chad, only half-joking.

"Wow, dude, that's a relief. I was kinda still sketched out

about the whole thing myself. I don't think Poo knows. Maybe one of us should call him?," suggests Jason.

"Yeah, you can tell Snoop Dog he beat the murder rap."

Travis picks up the phone and relays the news to Poo, encouraging him to come over and spend the day with the rest of us. He agrees.

"So, what up for today fellas?," asks Jason.

"I really oughta start packin' guys. Travis, you packed and ready to go?"

"Yeah, 'cept for little stuff here and there. Why don't you pack tomorrow?"

"If I agree to hang out today, no drugs guys, seriously. No pill in my drink, no paper on my tongue, no do-"

"We already chatted about that Dan. We feel the same way. It's gonna be a while before we all see each other again and we want to remember these last couple days."

"Did you guys have something specific in mind?"

"Of course." Chuck E. MUHPHUCKIN Cheeeeeese.

Inside, we order a shitload of pizza and grab as many tokens as we can carry. There's something so soothing to my ears about the sound of video games, especially the old school games, they really take me back..

Punch-out—"Body blow, Body blow."

Pole Position—"Prepare to Qualify."

A little comb rock-n-roll on Track and Field somewhere in the distance.

Right on. Good plan.

Chuckie's animatronic band is rocking out in the back room..*well come on baby, let's do the twist, just take me by the hand and go like this*..Poo is trashed, bought a round of beers with his fake ID and now he's heckling the band, and they aren't talking back so he quickly becomes disinterested and starts doing the twist; God help us all.

For the first time all week, I'm actually here with the guys, my mind actually present. We're not just spending time together, but actually enjoying each other's company, our heads in the moment.

I've been so self absorbed recently I completely forgot how much I care about them, each one of them. Jason. Poo. Chad. Travis. I've got love for the whole package too, for us, the crew. I can't help but feel guilty too though. It's not just my mother that would be upset if anything were to happen to me. What about the crew? And how would I feel if something happened to one of them? And how many times did I stand by idly this week while they endangered themselves? And others?

Right there amongst the maniacal laugh of the Sinistar, the frenzied whir of Pac-Man gobbling up dots and a soulful, robotic rendition of *Blue Suede Shoes*, I start promising myself things. To kick drugs. To practice what I preach. To be there for my mother. To start making a difference. To mind the flow and start living the plan. To spread the word.

Kill your television. Refuse subculture identification. Defy addiction. Cherish your individuality. Rise up.

Danny Boyle, Junior Revolutionary and Armchair Radical. I laugh out loud. At myself. As I often do.

After about ten rounds of best two out of three in *Mortal Kombat*, and a nice run at the *Gauntlet*, Travis and Poo decide it might be best to start heading home. I happen to agree as I'm late for my *appointment* with my mom.

On the way home I find myself struggling with whether or not I should come out to her or not. I want her to know, but I have no illusions about how she might react to finding out that her only son is gay. I think my father probably would have disowned me. Soon it's just me and Travis.

"Penny for your thoughts?," he asks, pulling one from his change holder.

159

"I'm going to tell my mom. About you. About us...me," I say rigidly.

He leans over to kiss me on the cheek, smiles and grabs my leg with his free hand, and it feels right, like it never has before. Without even thinking about it, I have just validated every second look, every word, smile, kiss and touch we've ever shared.

"You will never know how happy that makes me," he says. And I want to cry, because I'm finally in a position to make Travis happy, which is all I ever wanted in the first place.

"Me too," I say sheepishly, squeezing his hand tightly. "Me too."

The rest of the way home we carry on like lunatics, the radio cranked, belting out Circle Jerk tunes at the top of our lungs..*fuck me, teenage, I'm electric*..pounding our fists on the dashboard, exchanging smiles, acting stupid and being young. It's like a scene from one of those cheesy, post-grunge slacker films, but it's *us*, and so it works. My mom is waiting for me at the kitchen table when I get home. "Hey ma."

"Hey. I wasn't sure if you were going to make it."

"I'm sorry if I've seemed kind of distant this week. I've had a lot on my mind with going away to school and all," I say, taking a seat beside her.

"It's O.K. Dan. I understand."

Why does she have to be so understanding all the time? I could use a good, wholesome ass whipping every once in a while. "No it's not all right ma. I wish we could have spent more time together. I've been selfish, it's my bad."

"O.K., well then apology accepted."

I just can't win. Scream at me and tell me how unappreciative I am, how you bore me in your womb for nine months and this is the thanks you get, how spoiled I am, how if Dad were here he'd throw a fit, anything..nothing...I *have* to tell her.

"You're not allowed to accept it. Isn't a beating in order?"

"A beating? Dan, I've never laid a finger on you, I-"
"Well, you have to do something. Maybe ground me or-"
"Ground you? You're 18 years old Danny. I haven't grounded you in years."
"Well, do a symbolic grounding then. Just say, Danny, no television and no phone this week," hoping that a little humor will prepare her - I *must* tell her.
"Danny you're leaving on Friday."
"I know ma, I know. It's just symbolic like I said. I gotta flush this guilt so I can start fresh," I say, closing my eyes and tilting my head back. "Go on."
"No television and no phone this week for you young man."
"Ahh, much better," I say opening my eyes.
"You are too much," she says, chuckling.

Come out to my mom? Two days ago I wouldn't have considered that even in my wildest dreams and now here I am, the g-word hanging from the tip of my tongue, "Mom, I'm gay and I'm in love with Travis," I meant to just rehearse it, but it bailed on me, free-falling into the discussion. A hushed silence falls across the room as she lowers her eyes to the table.

Maybe I should have waited for a better time. We're both under a lot of pressure right now with me going away to school and all. She's quiet and contemplative.. mad crazy stress as I sit and await the verdict.

When she looks up, she appears to be in a lot of pain, her lip quivering, tears forming in her eyes. I always feared that she wouldn't be able to accept it, but I never thought it would hurt her. I hate to see my mother cry, and she's sobbing heavily now, standing to get a tissue. "Mom, I'm sorry," I blurt.
"It's not you, baby."
"What is it?"
Hand on the kitchen counter, she lifts her eyes to the window.
"Your father was gay."

"What?!" She nods, fighting back more tears.

I am completely floored. Never in a million years would I have thought for one second that my father was gay -

"Dad was gay?"

"He hated himself for it."

My dad. Gay. This is almost too much.

"But you two were married fo-"

"I couldn't just leave him," she says solemnly.

"But he taught me how to pitch, ma...how to bait a hook..to..," and then I realize what I'm saying and I'm ashamed.

"Just like you would teach your boy to do," she says, driving the point home. "Your father fought those stereotypes his whole life, Dan."

"How come no one ever told me? Maybe we could have talked about it...maybe he would have found some comfort in knowing that he wasn't alone."

"Danny, your father was very set in his ways."

"I could have helped. I could have been there for him," I insist.

"I knew your father almost better than he knew himself..and it wouldn't have made a difference. The only reason I am even telling you is because I don't want you to end up like he did, feeling like an outcast...like you have to drink yourself to sleep every night." If she only knew.

"That's why dad drank?"

"Yes. It helped him forget...who he was."

"When did he tell you?"

"On our fifth anniversary, after I threatened to leave him if he didn't stop drinking."

"I can't believe it."

She walks over to me and puts her hand on my shoulder, pulling my face against her stomach. "I love you Danny. So much..."

"I love you too," I say.

"..and that's never going to change."

And then I cry. It comes in waves, like I'm long over-due, and my mom just stands quietly and strokes my head. As the sobbing subsides, the phone rings. It's Travis. My mom looks at me sympathetically, questioning me with her eyes. I nod my head and take the phone.

"Hey.."

"You ready to do this, bro?," he asks enthusiastically.

"Yeah," I say, wiping my nose. My mom hands me a tissue and I walk into the next room.

"You get all your shit taken care of?"

"Yeah, I'm set."

"How did things go with your mom?" I turn and look back to the kitchen. She's pulling pans out of the cupboard and pre-paring the table for dinner.

"My mom rocks my world dude. I don't know what I'd do without her."

"You told her?"

"Yeah.. I told her."

"What did she say?"

"I'll tell you all about it tomorrow."

"Fair enough..hey, is everything straight between us?," I ask.

"I don't know if I'd use that word, but.." he laughs, "..yeah, we're straight."

"Whatever," we say in unison and I manage a laugh.

"See you bright and early then?"

"Yeah.."

"Okie then, Travis signing off."

"Goodnight stud."

"Goodnight Danny."

I dream that I'm at a club, and there's a lot of men standing around holding each other's hands. They're dancing and kissing. I'm standing alone in the corner, observing from afar.

There's a man sitting at the bar and he's staring at me,

smiling. He grabs a stool, pulling it up alongside of him, patting it with his hand. I walk over slowly.... "Hey sport."
"Hi," I stammer, looking around uneasily.

He opens his arms wide and I look at him hesitantly, studying his face. It's familiar, but..."Dad?"
"Come here, bud," and my defenses drop, falling into his arms and hugging him tightly.

I pull away and look at his face again. It's young, like he might have looked in his early twenties.
"Long time, no see," he says quaintly, and then I hug him again, tighter.
"I guess your mother told you, huh?"

I nod and put my head on his chest like when I was a little boy. There's so many things I want to say, but the moment seems so fleeting all ready.
"I'm sorry. I never meant to keep anything from you."
"I know," I say, letting go and taking a seat on the stool. My feet don't reach the floor. My hands are tiny.
"I love you, son. So does your mother. We still have a very good relationship, your mother and I...she's an amazing lady. I wish I could have given her the love and life that she deserves." He looks around contemplatively.
"I always told you to be true to yourself, son...I didn't have the strength."
"Why didn't you tell me?"
"I thought it didn't matter. I thought that if I held it all in, I was only failing myself...but in the end, I failed everybody. It's an incredibly selfish way to live, Dan. The world *needs* you, and the world needs you exactly as you are."
He looks sullenly at his drink.
"It's an illusion," he says, folds of his shirt shimmering like he's about to fade.
"You? This place?," I ask.
"No. This.." he says, raising his glass, dissolving in front of my eyes.

"Dad, wait.."
He turns to me, the image solidifying briefly, hanging in the air.
"I love you too," I say loudly.
He smiles and then he is gone.

On the wind
I hear the screams
of generations of tortured souls,
the agony of lives unlived,
the humanness of mortality
and the sorrow of a new day.

On the wind
I hear the plaintive wail
of a small baby crying,
the obsolescence of its future,
the path of its tears,
and innocence unknown.

On the wind
I hear the promises
that our ancestors made to us,
the nobleness of their cause,
the sacrifices that they made
and the world that has forgotten them.

On the wind
I hear the cost of ignorance,
the walls that it builds,
the hatred that it breeds,
the lives that it forfeits
and the pain that it brings.

On the wind
I hear the questions,
and the absence of answers,
the inverse of infinity,
the exactness of nothingness,
and the destructiveness of self-pity.

And on the wind I hear the call,
a call to revolution,
to the quest for knowledge,
the courage of the righteous,
the praise of the healthy
and care of the weak,
to the wisdom of our elders,
the strength of our convictions,
the gift of hope,
and the power of the human spirit.

On the wind

Peace and love,
Danny